*For Patrick (again), because
every time I stand at the entrance
of that dark cave, you are the
one beside me, holding my hand.*

First American Edition 2019
Kane Miller, A Division of EDC Publishing

*Polly and Buster: The Mystery of the Magic Stones*
Text & illustration copyright © 2018 Sally Rippin
Series design copyright © 2018 Hardie Grant Egmont
First published in Australia by Hardie Grant Egmont

Kane Miller, A Division of EDC Publishing
P.O. Box 470663
Tulsa, OK 74147-0663
**www.kanemiller.com**
**www.edcpub.com**
**www.usbornebooksandmore.com**

Library of Congress Control Number: 2018958207

Printed and bound in the United States of America
3 4 5 6 7 8 9 10
ISBN: 978-1-61067-927-5

# Polly AND Buster

## The Mystery of the Magic Stones

written & illustrated by

## SALLY RIPPIN

**Kane Miller**
A DIVISION OF EDC PUBLISHING

# What Came Before Now

Polly Proggett and Buster Grewclaw are the very best of friends. But Polly is a witch and Buster is a monster, and in Blackmoon Coven witches and monsters just don't mix.

Polly and Buster have managed to keep their friendship a secret so far – until one fateful day, on a school field trip to the gallery, when Polly accidentally unleashes a spell to protect Buster from his classmates, who are bullying him. Polly is terrified other witches will find out she is friendly with monsters and begs her teacher, Miss Spinnaker, to help keep her secret.

However, Deidre Halloway, head of the Committee, tells everyone that Polly did the spell to protect her daughter, Malorie, and that the monsters in the gallery are *dangerous*. Polly is celebrated as a hero, and so she goes along with the story.

But Polly's newfound popularity and this small untruth come with a terrible price.

A *Witches Against Monsters* movement begins to form, led by Mrs. Halloway, and quickly spreads throughout the town. Polly and Buster manage to escape Mrs. Halloway and her followers in the nick of time, and now they are hiding out in Miss Spinnaker's little kitchen, too frightened to return home.

Polly knows it's her fault that Buster has gotten caught up in Mrs. Halloway's horrible plan. She knows if Mrs. Halloway can convince enough witches that Buster is *dangerous*, the Mayor may agree to banish all monsters from Blackmoon Coven, for good!

How can Polly fix the trouble she has created? All she has are some magic stones, the faith of her teacher, and her very best friend by her side …

# One

Polly sits at her teacher's kitchen table and thinks about what lies ahead. She knows she is going to have to be braver than she has ever been. And cleverer than she has ever been. But frankly, she would rather be home in bed.

"Does it *have* to be me?" she asks her teacher.

She didn't mean for her voice to come out quite so **grumpy**, but her head is hurting and her hand is hurting and it *has* been a *very* long day. Escaping a fury of crazed witches and being bitten on the hand by a frightened monster aren't exactly the things that make you want to take on the world when you're only nine years old.

Polly rests her sore hand on the table and closes her eyes. The potion Miss Spinnaker has dabbed onto the bite has calmed the throbbing, and the swelling is beginning to disappear. When she opens her eyes again she sees her teacher looking at her kindly.

"I'm afraid so, Polly," Miss Spinnaker says. "It's true it's a little surprising the stones have chosen someone quite as —" she pauses as she considers her words carefully, "well, *inexperienced* as you, but we must trust them. They will tell you what to do. Don't worry. I am here and I will help you as best I can."

**"Me too!"** says Buster eagerly. He wipes ju-ju fruit juice from his chin with his big, hairy paw. "I am brave and strong and I would absolutely **love** to be part of an adventure."

Polly sighs. Only a few days ago her life was so predictably ordinary. Normally, at this time of night, she would be snuggled up next to her mother watching TV, their pet bortal snoring on the rug and her older sister, Winifred, picking at her black nail polish in the beanbag in front of them. Instead, she is hiding out in her teacher's little cottage with her best friend, while a nasty gaggle of witches is out there looking for them.

*That's what you get for trying to be a hero,* she grumbles to herself, and for a moment Polly regrets having stood up for her oldest and dearest friend when he was being bullied in the gallery for showing his feelings. But when she looks at Buster, who is smiling at her **goofily** with a purple smear of ju-ju juice across his chin, she knows she never really had a choice. Friends stand up for friends, no matter what. There's no two ways about it.

"All right," she says, taking a big, deep breath to fill her tummy with courage. She picks the stones up off the table and tucks them back into her pocket. "So, what's our plan?"

Buster whoops with excitement.

Miss Spinnaker smiles. "Well, first of all, I think we should let your parents know you are safe." She stands up, gently easing her sleek black cat off her lap. It skulks into the corner, looking annoyed at being woken from its slumber. "They must be worried sick by now. I suggest we do a quick spin past on the broomstick to check in with them and maybe pick up some pajamas and your toothbrushes.

You can stay here tonight, if you're allowed, until we figure out what to do next."

*A sleepover!* Polly's heart soars. *And another broomstick ride!* The **fizzy excitement** of their last ride, when Miss Spinnaker rescued them from the clock tower, still buzzes through her. Now their adventure is beginning to seem more appealing.

But when Polly looks across at Buster, she sees her friend has turned a paler shade of green.

"Oh," Buster says, his mouth curling into a worried little grimace. "I guess it's not a real and proper adventure if we just *walk* there, right?"

Polly laughs. "What happened to big, brave Buster, not scared of anything?"

"I'm *not* scared of anything," Buster frowns. "I just get a little airsick, that's all."

"I'll fly gently," Miss Spinnaker assures them, and she bustles about, sweeping things into a midnight blue velvet bag she has slung over her shoulder.

Polly watches her teacher stride over to a tall glass cabinet where a collection of various witch things are on display. Miss Spinnaker stands in front of it, hesitating for a moment, before unclipping a long brass wand from its hook and tucking it into her bag.

Polly's stomach tightens. "You're bringing a *wand*?" she whispers, glancing about as though someone might hear her.

Miss Spinnaker turns to face Polly, and her eyes glitter. "Polly, this is not a **game**," she says in a low voice.

Polly reaches for Buster's paw. She feels it shrink a little in her own as the **seriousness** of their adventure washes over them.

Buster clears his throat. "I'm not scared," he says, his voice cracking. "No, not me. Not one bit!"

"Me neither," says Polly loudly, mainly to reassure Buster. She knows that until everything in their town is back to normal, it is up to her to keep him safe.

"It's OK to be scared," Miss Spinnaker says. "To be afraid of something and do it anyway is the mark of true courage. And that is something you both have in **cauldron loads**.

All right, my lovelies, let's go!"

She swishes past them toward the front door, cape billowing and bracelets jangling.

# Two

The midnight sky is spattered with stars and the moon shines gently on the three figures huddled onto Miss Spinnaker's broomstick as they glide through the *velvety night*.

Polly's cheeks and hands sting with the cold, but her back is warm against her teacher's chest and her mouth is dry from grinning. She wonders how Buster is doing at the back, holding on tightly, his eyes squeezed shut, but doesn't dare turn around in case she loses her balance. Being on the front of a broomstick, so high in the sky, is the most **thrilling feeling** Polly has ever known.

Polly sees the lights of Blackmoon Coven twinkling beneath them and, for a moment, all her problems seem as small and far away as this tiny world. She wishes she could stay up here forever and never have to face the mess she has made.

But just as this thought passes through her mind, her tummy drops as they begin their descent.

**"Oh,"** Buster groans.

"Sorry," Miss Spinnaker calls out, and tips up the front of the broomstick handle so they ease down more gently.

Polly recognizes her street and soon her and Buster's identical houses, side by side, one neat and one shabby, with the old morpett tree in her backyard stretching out its branches between them. This is the tree that hid their friendship for years until that unfortunate day in the gallery.

Ever since then, everything has gone from bad to worse. Polly wishes things were like they were before. She feels a sudden need to hug her mother and realizes she can't remember the last time she told her she loved her.

They cruise closer, almost near enough to touch the roof tiles, when Polly feels the broomstick lurch sideways. The houses spin away from them and Miss Spinnaker flattens against her as she picks up speed.

# "Hold on tight!"

she yells, and Polly feels the sharpness of her teacher's voice cut deep into her chest.

"What's happening?" Polly calls, her heart yammering.

Miss Spinnaker hisses into Polly's hair. "Look behind you!"

Polly **grips** the wooden handle **tightly** and dares a **peek** over her shoulder.

What she sees makes her gasp. A flock of witches on broomsticks, maybe a dozen, are closing in on them. Even though Polly only catches a glimpse, she instantly recognizes the snaky, silvery hair of Mrs. Halloway, who is leading the pack.

**"Ohhhh ..."** Buster groans weakly.

"I'm sorry, Buster, you'll just have to hold on!" Miss Spinnaker yells, as she swerves suddenly upward.

Even Polly has to close her eyes as the ground swirls far beneath them, and her stomach drops into her toes. When she opens them again, she is horrified to see Mrs. Halloway drawing closer. Within moments, the furious witch is almost beside them. Her lips curl back into a sneer, and she reaches into her cape.

"Go faster!" Polly yells, but she can feel Miss Spinnaker's old wooden broomstick straining under the weight of them.

There is no way they can outrace a mad, mean witch on a Silver 500.

"**Deidre!**" Miss Spinnaker yells into the wind. "You know the rules. No wands in the presence of children!"

"**Those old rules no longer matter, Iris,**" Mrs. Halloway snarls. "Now that monsters have become a threat to witches, we must do what we can to defend ourselves."

"**Don't be ridiculous!**" Miss Spinnaker yells. "Buster is an innocent monster. He poses no threat to anyone."

She jerks the broomstick to the right, but Mrs. Halloway has no trouble catching up to them.

"You have to choose, Iris!" Mrs. Halloway says, coming in close enough for Polly to see her mean black eyes narrowing. Her hair whips wildly in the wind. "Don't you know? It's **Witches Against Monsters** now. Toss that dangerous monster off the back of your broomstick and prove your loyalty to witches. You can save yourself – or nobody."

Buster whimpers.

"**No!**" Polly screeches. "Don't do it, Miss Spinnaker."

"Oh, Polly," Miss Spinnaker hisses. "Who do you think I am?" She raises her voice. "Deidre Halloway, how *dare* you threaten me! I am the Head of Spells at your very own daughter's school. You will never get away with this!"

Mrs. Halloway cackles. "No one can see us up here," she says, gesturing to the flock of witches becoming lost in the swirl of silver clouds behind them. "Accidents on broomsticks happen all time. Especially at this height. And who is everyone going to believe anyway? A couple of pathetic **monster** lovers? Or the head of the Committee? It's over, Iris. The time of monsters freely roaming the streets is gone." And with that, she pulls out her wand from her flapping cape and

points

it at

Buster.

"Miss Spinnaker!" Polly yells, but her teacher already has her heavy brass wand in her hand.

A spark erupts from the tip of Mrs. Halloway's wand

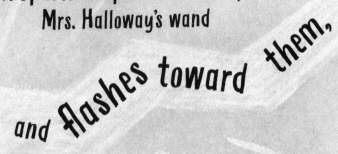

and flashes toward them,

but Miss Spinnaker deflects it with an electric green flash of her own. The broomstick wobbles dangerously and Buster groans again.

"Polly! You'll have to steer the stick," Miss Spinnaker yells.

"What?" Polly gasps. "But I've never …"

"Just steer!"

# Three

Polly plants her hands firmly on the wooden
handle and tries to remember what she knows
about broomstick flying. Apparently it's all
in the weight of your body, she remembers
her sister telling her, and she leans abruptly
to the left. The broomstick swerves and Miss
Spinnaker falls hard against her.

"Gently!" her teacher yells. "And don't
look down."

Of course this last bit of advice only serves to make Polly look down, and she sees the ground spinning up to meet them. Her stomach **lurches.** Miss Spinnaker pulls Polly tightly against her and, as she leans backward, the broomstick lifts skyward again.

"**I want to get off,**" Buster moans. But both Polly and Miss Spinnaker ignore him.

Polly leans to the right and they peel away toward a line of trees in the opposite direction, inky black against the navy sky.

"Good thinking, Polly," Miss Spinnaker says. "Keep going straight. That's the Amber Skull Forest up ahead."

Polly feels her chest **fill with pride.**

She thinks she might be beginning to get the hang of this broomstick-flying business.

Mrs. Halloway jerks her broomstick around **and sends another jolt in their direction,** but this time Miss Spinnaker is prepared. She spins her wrist in circles and throws out a twisting bolt of light just as Mrs. Halloway's spark nearly hits them. The spark bounces off Miss Spinnaker's well-timed bolt and spirals into the night. The dark forest looms ahead.

"What should I do?" Polly yells.

"Just keep going," Miss Spinnaker yells back.

They enter the forest, crashing through branches and leaves, then Polly hears a roar of flames rise up behind her. She feels a searing heat against her back.

"Don't stop," Miss Spinnaker shouts. "And whatever you do, don't look behind you."

This time, Polly does what she is told, and they zigzag through the trees while the forest is devoured by flames.

Polly feels her heart sink. She knows the wall of fire will protect them from Mrs. Halloway and her cronies, but she feels deeply saddened that a whole forest needed to die just to save them.

"Don't worry," Miss Spinnaker murmurs into her ear, as if she's read Polly's mind. "An illusion spell can look and feel so much like the real thing even grown witches have been known to be fooled."

Polly gasps. An illusion spell! Her teacher never ceases to impress her, but she had no idea she was *this* powerful.

Miss Spinnaker takes over directing the handle and slows the broomstick down to its former speed. They chug through the forest a few feet above the leafy floor. All around them forest animals **screech, swing and flutter** through the trees in fear of the burning wall of fire. Even though the flames are no longer rolling toward them, it still **belches out clouds of black smoke.** Polly takes in a deep lungful and discovers it tastes of fresh air.

"It will dissolve soon," Miss Spinnaker reassures her. "The animals will be OK." She pats Polly's arm. "Good work with the broomstick flying. If I didn't know better I'd think you'd done it all your life."

"Thanks, Miss Spinnaker," Polly grins, her

heart pounding and her hands clammy on the broomstick handle.

Polly hears Buster moan. "Are we there yet?" he groans weakly. "My tummy hurts."

"Just a little longer," Miss Spinnaker soothes.

"Are we still going back to your place?" Polly asks Miss Spinnaker. She twists around to see Buster leaning his whole weight against her teacher. His eyes are shut, his long arms are draped around her neck, and he has shrunk into a tight, furry ball. *Dear old Buster*, she thinks. *He's the bravest monster I know and he's afraid of heights!*

"No, not now," Miss Spinnaker says. "Now that Deidre Halloway knows you are with me she will likely be heading straight to my house. We can't go there."

Polly feels a worm of worry in her belly. "Where will we go then?"

"I'm taking you somewhere safe," says Miss Spinnaker. "It's not far off now. See that little light through the trees?"

Polly squints and, sure enough, sees a pale yellow glow in the distance. "Who in blinking bats would live *there*?" she asks.

"That, Polly, my dear," says Miss Spinnaker, sighing deeply, "is my mother's house."

# *Four*

iss Spinnaker pulls up in front of a small
stone hut, built into the mound of a grassy
hill and completely hidden by trees.

Polly feels her heart **butterfly** with curiosity.
Miss Spinnaker's *mother*! She knows that teachers
have homes and parents and all those sorts of
things, but it still feels very strange to think of

Miss Spinnaker having a life outside of school. When Polly was little she even thought her teachers *lived* at school!

Buster tumbles off his end of the broomstick and curls into a ball. **"Oh, my tummy,"** he wails. **"I don't feel good."**

Polly giggles. "But you are always floating up into the sky, Buster! You shouldn't be afraid of heights."

Buster frowns. "It's not the *height*, Polly, it's the speed. And anyway, I told you, I'm not *scared*. Just airsick."

"Come along, Buster," Miss Spinnaker says, smiling kindly. "We'll find something inside to fix you up."

Polly skips along a stepping-stone path with her teacher, patting her pocket to check the stones are still there. It winds through the dark and shadowy suggestion of a vegetable garden.

"Are you sure your mother will be all right with us turning up this late at night?" she asks. She looks back at Buster, still lying on the grass, and lowers her voice. "And with a ... you know ... *monster*?"

Miss Spinnaker stops and turns to face Polly, a wry smile on her face. "Don't worry. My mother has so few guests she'd welcome *anyone* I bring into this home. Witch *or* monster." She calls out to Buster, who is clutching his stomach and groaning. "Come along now, Buster. Stop making a fuss. We won't wait out in the cold for you all evening."

Miss Spinnaker walks up to the heavy wooden door and reaches for the solid brass knocker, molded into the shape of a monster's fist. But before she has the chance to grasp it, the door swings open and the front porch is flooded with warm light.

"Iris!" comes a husky little voice.

Polly stares at Miss Spinnaker's mother, who is not at all what she expected. Her teacher has proven to be no end of surprises over the past twenty-four hours, but somehow Polly had imagined Miss Spinnaker, Head of Spells and powerful Black Witch, to have a rather grand and imposing mother, a little like the headmistress at Miss Madden's Academy.

Instead, the witch at the front door is squat and round. She has frizzy dyed hair that puffs out from her scalp like a pink cloud, and a big stain down the front of her baggy floral nightdress.

When she sees who is hiding behind her daughter, she smiles, and Polly notices she has several teeth missing.

# "Ooh, how delightful!"

she coos. "You've brought me some visitors!"

"We're not staying long," Miss Spinnaker says. "Just for a night or two, that's all. Polly and her friend are … er … in a little bit of trouble with the Committee."

"Well, come in! Come in!" Miss Spinnaker's mother says. "Plenty of room in here. Mortimer!" she yells. "We've got guests. You'll have to make up the beds in the spare room."

Polly follows Miss Spinnaker into the little stone house. "Mortimer?" she asks. "Is he your dad?" She wonders why her teacher hasn't mentioned him before.

Miss Spinnaker shakes her head. "No. Kind of. It's complicated. Hurry up, Buster," she calls out, and marches ahead of Polly down the corridor.

Polly feels a little **giggle of excitement bubble up through her**. Even in her wildest dreams, she never would have imagined doing all the things she's done tonight. A dangerous broomstick chase, a Fire Illusion spell in the woods, and even meeting her teacher's *parents*. Polly is beginning to like this adventure already.

"Come on, Buster," she calls out, walking back to help her best friend to his feet. "You'll be OK in a little while."

Polly grabs Buster's paw and manages to pull him into a wobbly upright position. He is still as small as Polly and a sickly shade of gray.

Suddenly his eyes grow wide. His cheeks puff out and he claps his paw over his mouth. But it's no use. Half-eaten ju-ju berries **spray through his fingers,** narrowly missing Polly's feet.

"Ew, Buster!" she squeals, jumping backward in disgust.

"Oh," Buster groans, wiping the sticky juice off his fur. The color begins to return to his face and he puffs out to his normal size again. "That's better. That's *much* better." He wipes a paw across his mouth, then starts to walk toward the door. "Come on then!" he says.

Polly laughs, skipping away from the puddle of mushed-up ju-ju fruits.

"You know what?" Buster says, putting on his very serious voice. "I think I may have learned something tonight."

Polly rolls her eyes at him. "What's that?" she giggles.

Buster grins. He puts a paw on Polly's shoulder and bends down toward her. Polly jerks back a little, her nose wrinkling at the smell of fermented fruit on his breath.

Buster shakes his head and strokes his big hairy stomach. "Ju-ju fruits and broomstick rides. Just. Don't. Mix."

# Five

Miss Spinnaker's mother leads them into a round kitchen with a huge fireplace that yawns like a big sooty mouth along one wall. Something that smells like soup is simmering in the blackened iron cauldron, and there is a lump of spickleseed bread wrapped in cloth in a basket on the worn wooden table.

"You poor popkins must be hungry," she says in her high, raspy voice. She ties a grubby apron around her waist and unhooks a big ladle from near the fireplace.

Buster opens his mouth to speak, but Polly cuts him off. "No, just tired, Mrs. … um … *Spinnaker*?"

"Call me Flora, dear," Miss Spinnaker's mother says, smiling her toothless smile and stroking Polly's head with her big, rough hand.

"Er … Flora," Polly tries out. It feels very weird to call her teacher's mother by her first name.

"Yes, bed for these two," Miss Spinnaker says firmly. She gestures to the shiny brass clock on the mantlepiece, shaped like a bortal, and Polly sees it is already well past midnight. Suddenly every bone in her body aches from tiredness and she misses her mother more than ever. It's been a *very* long day.

"Beds are ready," comes a deep, rolling voice from the hall, and Polly turns to the doorway to catch a glimpse of Miss Spinnaker's father.

But when he steps into the kitchen, she gasps.

Polly looks at Miss Spinnaker, then at Buster. His mouth has dropped open, too.

"Polly, Buster," Miss Spinnaker says, in a strange voice Polly hasn't heard her use before, "this is Mortimer. My *step*father."

Mortimer **crosses** the kitchen in three **enormous paces** and scoops Polly up into his big hairy arms. Then he kisses her loudly on both cheeks.

Polly feels her body grow stiff as a board.

Miss Spinnaker's stepfather is a *monster*.

# "Wonderful to meet you!"

he says grandly, a huge smile stretching out his big rubbery lips.

Then he wraps his arms around Miss Spinnaker and Buster and gives them both a **monster-sized hug,** too.

Polly can't speak. All her words are caught up in a knot in the back of her throat and all she can do is smile awkwardly.

"All right, bedtime now," Miss Spinnaker says, noticing Polly's discomfort. She untangles herself from Mortimer's enthusiastic embrace. "There will be plenty of time for everyone to get to know each other tomorrow."

She takes Polly and Buster's hands and leads them out of the kitchen to a little room just off the hallway. Inside are two single beds, side by side, with a rickety wooden table in between. A pretty, tasseled lamp gives out a soft golden glow.

Buster climbs into one narrow bed, and Polly climbs into the other. Miss Spinnaker pulls the patchwork blanket up to Polly's chin, then perches on the end of her bed.

Even though Polly can barely keep her eyes open, her mind is racing.

"Your stepfather is a *monster*? But that's … that's *impossible*!"

Miss Spinnaker leans over and smooths Polly's knotty hair off her forehead. Polly can smell the midnight air in her robes.

"Polly," Miss Spinnaker says, in her gentlest voice. "You should know, more than anyone, it doesn't matter *who* you love. Just as long as you love."

She smiles, but there is a trace of sadness in her eyes that Polly doesn't understand. "Now, off to sleep," she says, and leans over to switch off the lamp. "We have lots to do tomorrow."

"Can we please let my mom know I'm OK?" Polly asks in a little voice. The hall light spills into the room and Polly can still make out her teacher's kind face in the shadows.

"Of course," Miss Spinnaker reassures her. "I'll send her a message on a nighthawk tonight and she'll get it as soon as she wakes."

Miss Spinnaker turns to check on Buster, but he is already fast asleep. She pulls his blanket up a little higher so that it covers his shoulders, then turns to head out of the room. "Good night, my lovelies," she says from the doorway.

"Wait!" says Polly.

Miss Spinnaker sighs. "Polly, it's late," she says, "and I'm very tired."

"Sorry," Polly mumbles. "But my mom always kisses me good night and says the Gorvan Spell. Do you think you could …?"

Miss Spinnaker wanders back over to Polly. She plants a gentle kiss on her forehead, then whispers,

*"Darkling day, drifting light*
*Keep you safe all through the night.*
*Sleep my child, your dreams are sound*
*While the gorvan's underground."*

Then she touches the three points of Polly's face – her forehead, her nose and her chin – with her two middle fingers. "You know the gorvan's not real, don't you?" she says.

"I know," says Polly, shrugging. "I just like my mom to say it to me. It reminds me of my dad. He used to say it every night when he tucked me into bed."

"Mine too," says Miss Spinnaker, smiling. "Now, it really is time for you to sleep. Your friend over here obviously has no trouble in that department." She gestures toward Buster, who is snoring loudly.

Polly giggles. "I know. He doesn't seem to worry about stuff as much as I do."

"That's OK. That just means you have a good imagination," Miss Spinnaker tells her. "Now, how about you listen to Buster's snores and imagine you're on a boat on a rumbling sea, rocking you to sleep. Can you try that?"

"I'll try," says Polly, and she closes her eyes.

She listens to Miss Spinnaker leave the room and does her best to bring the image of a rumbling sea into her mind.

But it is no use. Sleep just won't come.

# Six

Polly lies awake in the dark for what feels like hours listening to Buster's snores. She tosses this way and that, but the magic stones in her pocket seem to be getting hotter, as if they are trying to tell her something.

She sits up in bed, pulls out the little silk pouch and tips them into her palm. They *gleam gently* in the dark: one pink, one blue and one amber.

The amber one glows the brightest and when Polly peers at the little eye shape inside the stone, it seems to be watching her.

*What do you want?* she wonders.

She is not sure if she is brave enough to ask them. The first time was so frightening – and that was with Miss Spinnaker by her side! Does she dare do it again? And on her own? But the stones are burning so brightly now Polly knows she doesn't have a choice.

Polly closes her fingers over the stones and shuts her eyes. Immediately her mind fills with a vision. She sees a shadowy place: a long, cold tunnel, dark and spooky. It pulls her toward it, but the closer she gets, the heavier she feels, until her whole body seems as heavy as boulders. A thick purple fog **oozes** its way out of the tunnel toward her, curling around her feet.

Suddenly, the stones become too hot to hold and Polly tips them onto the bedding. But just as she opens her eyes, one last image flashes into her mind. It's a face she knows, hazy but familiar. Terribly, heart-achingly familiar. A sob bursts from her chest.

"Papa!" she breathes softly into the night.

She understands where that place is now, that long, spooky tunnel burrowing deep into the ground. It's the Hollow Valley Mines. The place where her father is buried. That's where the stones want her to go.

Polly tips the stones back into the pouch, cool again now they have passed on their message, and tucks them back into her pocket. She feels too shaken to try to sleep now, and this dark house full of strangers does little to comfort her. So she swings her bare feet down onto the cold stone floor and pads out into the hallway to look for Miss Spinnaker. She hopes her teacher might still be awake.

"Miss Spinnaker?" Polly calls into the dark.

Noisy snoring comes from a bedroom at the end of the corridor. One snore is deep, low and rumbling, the other high and squeaky.

Polly sees a yellow glow coming from underneath a door on her left. "Miss Spinnaker?" she calls again, a little more loudly this time, inching toward the door. It swings open and light spills out into the hallway.

"Polly?" says Miss Spinnaker, her wild red hair all a tumble, lit up by the fireplace in the room behind her. She is wearing a fluffy pink dressing gown that Polly immediately guesses to be Flora's, as the sleeves are way too short for her, and Miss Spinnaker *really* doesn't seem to be the fluffy pink dressing gown type.

"What are you doing out of bed?" Her teacher's voice sounds cross at first, but when she sees Polly's bottom lip tremble, she takes her hand, closes the door behind them, and leads her into the living room to sit by the fire.

"Oh, sweetie. Did you have a bad dream?" she says, stroking Polly's tangled hair. "Here, why don't you sit with me for a while?"

Polly leans into the warmth of her favorite teacher, who smells of brindlewood and thyme. There is a pillow on the sofa, along with a rumpled blanket. Polly realizes this is where Miss Spinnaker has set herself up to sleep.

"I'm sorry, I didn't mean to disturb you," Polly says quietly.

"That's all right," Miss Spinnaker says. "I was actually just doing a bit of reading." She points to the chunky wooden coffee table in front of them, where there is a pile of books and magazines and a half-drunk cup of tea. "I don't sleep that well either."

Polly leans over to pick up a heavy book. The black leather cover is cracked and worn, and the gold lettering across the front has almost rubbed off with use.

"My old university spell book," Miss Spinnaker says, gently taking it from Polly and placing it back on the table. "You're not ready for that one." She pushes a couple of other heavy books to one side and pulls out a slim exercise book, similar to the ones Polly uses at school. "You can look at this one," she says, smiling. "Though it might be a bit embarrassing."

"What is it?" asks Polly, peering down at the cover. She gasps. "Was this from when you were at Miss Madden's?"

Miss Spinnaker nods. "My mother keeps everything. That's my grade five spell book.

Look at my marks. I was doing a lot worse than you when I was your age!"

Polly flicks through the pages. They are covered in scrawly writing in different-colored pens, and there are notes and diagrams and drawings, too. And Miss Spinnaker is not exaggerating. Her marks were terrible!

"How did you get to be Head of Spells at Miss Madden's when you did so badly at school?" Polly asks, amazed.

Miss Spinnaker points to the small, neat handwriting that appears at the bottom of each page. "Mrs. Blackfeather. Somehow she believed in me when no one else did. Even though my marks were bad, she always wrote encouraging comments for me. I would have dropped out of the Academy if it hadn't been for her. You see? It only took one person to believe in me." She pauses and takes Polly's bandaged hand in hers. "And even though I know you are scared and you are really not sure if you can do this, you have *lots* of people who believe in you, Polly. Many more than I ever did."

"Really?" says Polly, sticking out her bottom lip. "Who?" she insists, but only because she wants to hear Miss Spinnaker tell her.

"Oh, Polly!" Miss Spinnaker chuckles. "Me! Buster! Even your dad, in a way. He wouldn't have given you those stones if he didn't believe in you, Polly."

At the mention of her dad, Polly shrinks back into the couch and chews at her thumbnail.

"What is it, Polly? Is that what woke you? Did you have a dream about your dad?"

"Not really," Polly mumbles. She feels her cheeks burn. She's scared Miss Spinnaker will be angry if she admits she used the stones without her, but her teacher always seems to know when Polly isn't being completely honest.

"Tell me, Polly," she says kindly, her red hair *gleaming* in the firelight. "You've already learned the hard way that it's much simpler just to tell the truth from the beginning, before it becomes bigger and harder to control. I promise I won't get cross with you."

Polly breathes in deeply. Despite the roaring fire beside them, she shivers. "I used the stones," she mumbles, looking up at Miss Spinnaker. "I'm sorry! But it's like they were calling me." She looks down and fiddles with the cover of Miss Spinnaker's old spell book in her lap. "I think they want me to go to the Hollow Valley Mines," she whispers. "To find my dad."

"Oh, Polly!" Miss Spinnaker says, hugging Polly tightly. "That must have been very scary for you. But you must have misunderstood the stones. I know you wish you could see your dad again, but he's gone, Polly. It's been five years since the mine collapsed. Lots of witches and monsters lost loved ones that day, but nothing will bring them back again. Not even the most powerful magic can reverse death." She looks at Polly seriously. "You must promise me that you will never go near those mines, OK? They are too dangerous for a young witch like you. Even the Mayor has declared them out-of-bounds. You know that, Polly."

Polly nods, but she feels confused. She slips her fingers into her pocket to touch the pouch of stones. "But you told me to trust the stones …"

"Polly," Miss Spinnaker says firmly. "Until I can get you back to your families safely, you and Buster are my responsibility, stones or no stones. Look, I am going to head out early tomorrow morning to try to sort some things out and I want you to wait here for me until I return, all right? You'll be safe here. I won't be long, I promise. Mom and Mortimer will look after you. Then we'll work out how to get you home. Meanwhile, you and I need to get some sleep. We both have a long day ahead of us. Come along."

She stands up and takes Polly's hand, then leads her back along the dark hallway toward the bedroom.

"Here," Miss Spinnaker says. She opens up a small cupboard by the door and pulls out a brinket. She twists the top until it cracks and it lets out a *gentle pink glow*. Then she places it on the bedside table next to the lamp and pulls the blankets up to Polly's chin again. "Now, I want you asleep before that brinket has burnt out, OK?"

Polly nods. "OK."

"I'll be back right after breakfast. No more using those stones while I'm not around. You may well be a Silver Witch, but you're still only nine. And your mother would never forgive me if she knew I was responsible for putting any dangerous ideas into your head."

Miss Spinnaker plumps up Polly's pillow, then leans over and strokes her forehead. "Do you need me to do a sleeping spell over you?" she says gently.

"No, I'll be OK," Polly says. She shuffles her

hip a little where the stones are digging into her. It feels uncomfortable sleeping in her clothes and her teeth feel furry from not having been brushed, but now tiredness has well and truly taken over and she feels her eyelids growing heavy and sore.

"What happened to your dad?" Polly murmurs sleepily, trying to keep her teacher by her side for just a little longer.

"You are a nosy one, aren't you?" Miss Spinnaker says kindly, but there is sadness in her voice. "Let's just say my mother is a **hundred times happier** with Mortimer than she ever was with my father. Even if Mortimer *is* a monster. You know as well as I do that not all monsters are bad and not all witches and warlocks are good. Now, good night, Polly," she says, standing up and pulling the gaudy pink dressing gown more tightly around her.

But even before she has closed the door behind her, Polly has drifted off to sleep.

# Seven

Polly hears a low murmuring noise pulling her up through her dreams. The voice gets louder and louder.

## "Polleee. Polleeeee ..."

She opens one eye and then the other, her head still groggy with sleep. Buster is leaning right over her, peering into her face.

He has opened the curtains and pale sunlight streams in through the little round window. "Are you awake?" he asks hopefully.

"I am now!" Polly says, rubbing her eyes and yawning. "What time is it?"

"I don't know, but I'm hungry," Buster says. "Can you smell something?"

Polly giggles. "Right now all I can smell is your *breath*," she says, pulling the blanket back over her head.

Buster jerks Polly's blanket off her in one tug. "Aw, come on, Polly!" he says. "This is the first day of our adventure!"

Although she is still sleepy, Polly grins to see her very best friend at the end of her bed.

Buster is right. They have just had their first sleepover!

She scrambles out of bed and the two of them race to be first in the kitchen, where they find Flora already sitting at the table, a big pot of tea in front of her. She is dressed in a traditional witch smock, faded to gray, with a white lace collar and a bulky yellow knitted cardigan over the top. Her hair is a halo of frizzy pink. When she takes a sip of tea from her little bortal-shaped cup, Polly can smell lavender and bergamot and sunshine. Flora smiles at them as they run in and her cheeks bloom pink from the tea.

Mortimer is at the stove in a frilly apron and floral shorts, cooking something that smells amazing. Buster's tummy growls in appreciation.

"Just in time," Mortimer says. He places a massive stack of flipcakes in the middle of the table and drizzles them with syrup. Polly watches in amazement as it

**crackles and fizzes,**

shooting little sparks up to the ceiling.

"Sparkle syrup," Mortimer winks. "An old witch favorite of Flora's. Pull up a chair!"

"Oh, thank you." Buster sighs like he hasn't eaten a thing for days, and slides into a seat beside Polly.

"Has Miss Spinnaker left yet?" Polly asks, reaching for a flipcake. She dips her finger in a little of the syrup and is delighted to discover it tastes as fizzy as it looks. Her mother never cooks with magic ingredients anymore. Only boring foods like thistleweeds and mealworms.

"Oh yes," Flora chuckles. "Iris was up hours ago. Don't look like that, popkin! She won't be long. We'll have fun together this morning. Won't we, Mortimer?"

"You bet!" says Mortimer, tossing the frying pan in his great big paw so that the flipcakes **soar** into the air and land neatly back in the pan.

Polly knows her mother would freak if she found out she had been left in a house with a *monster*. Aside from Buster's family and the straggly bunch of monsters his mother takes in, Polly has never really spent much time with other monsters. She still finds it hard to believe Mortimer lives here. With Miss Spinnaker's *mother*!

"I *like* Mortimer," Buster whispers to Polly through mouthfuls of food, his lips **sparkling with syrup.** "He makes *very* good flipcakes."

Polly takes a bite. It's true. Mortimer's flipcakes are excellent. And she has never eaten anything quite as **wondrous** as Flora's sparkle syrup! Polly studies Miss Spinnaker's stepfather carefully as she eats. He is tall and lanky, with broad, hairy shoulders and massive hands and feet. He moves like a monster, with big sweeping gestures, and he has a booming monstery voice, but whenever he comes close to Flora, he almost always pauses to give her a toothy smile or plant a gentle kiss on her head. And when Flora looks back up at him, she blushes like a young witchling.

Polly knows her mother adored her father, but she doesn't remember them ever acting like this. **Like two bluebirds in love.** And the more Polly watches Flora and Mortimer together, the less weird it seems, until she has almost forgotten that Mortimer is a monster.

"Do you think I could use your phone to call my mom?" Polly asks, after she has finished breakfast. "She must be so worried by now!"

Flora looks at Polly, a smear of syrup on her chin. "Oh, we don't have anything fancy like that. Morty, imagine? Us having one of those phone-gadget thingies!" She snorts. "Who would we call anyway? No, we only have a broken-down crystal ball, which I use to keep an eye on my grandchildren. It doesn't tune well these days though. But don't worry. Iris sent a message on a nighthawk last night to let your parents know you're both safe. And you'll be home in no time. Now, why don't you go outside and play while you're waiting for her? Mortimer and I can tidy the kitchen. Go on, off you go!"

"All right," Polly says, dragging Buster from the table. He stares longingly at the few remaining flipcakes on the plate, swimming in sparkle syrup. "Come on, Buster. Let's go and find a good tree to climb."

# Eight

Polly and Buster run out the front door and find a morpett tree with wide, low branches that looks perfect for climbing. Buster **swings up easily** – his arms are long and strong – and once he finds a good hollow for them to nestle into, he pulls Polly up beside him. Mortimer waves at them from the kitchen window and they wave back.

The sun shines through the leaves and dapples their faces. They watch a speckled treeworm climb slowly up the trunk beside them. In the distance, the forest hums with the chatter

and chirrup of birds swooping in and out of the trees. "I like it here," Buster says, leaning back against the trunk of the tree, his paws behind his head. "I like Mortimer and Flora and of course having an adventure with *you*. But I do miss my mom. I hope Miss Spinnaker comes back soon so we can go home."

"Me too," says Polly. She leans against Buster. He is as **soft and comforting** as a favorite blanket and he smells like the trees. He begins to hum and she can feel the reverberation of his deep voice through his chest. It is their made-up song.

*"Me and you, you and me,
that's the way it will always be,"*

he croons, and Polly feels him expand with happiness.

*Dear old Buster*, she thinks. *It doesn't take much to make him happy. As long as he has a belly full of food and a tree to lie in.*

Sometimes Polly wishes she was as uncomplicated as Buster – more fun and less worry. But even now, when she should be feeling as carefree as he does, she can't help worrying about where Miss Spinnaker might be, and why she is taking so long, and, most importantly, how they are going to get Buster safely back to his family while those nasty witches are out there, looking for him.

*If only Malorie hadn't told her mother about Buster coming to my window,* Polly thinks crossly. She remembers how her classmate had almost convinced her they could be friends. *It's just silly that Mrs. Halloway thinks she can make other witches believe Buster is dangerous. I mean, just look at him! Buster is about the sweetest, kindest monster you could ever meet. Anyone with two eyes could see that!*

She looks at her old friend, stretched out along the tree branch, eyes closed and crooning happily, and smiles.

Just then, Polly hears a noise: a familiar buzzing sound coming from above that makes her skin prickle in fear.

"Shh!" she warns Buster, and puts a finger to her lips.

He stops singing and his eyes grow wide.

Polly listens again. She would know that sound anywhere. **It's the buzz of a SILVER 500**. The newest and most powerful broomstick around. And there is only one witch Polly knows who owns one of those.

## Mrs. Halloway!

Polly's heart begins to pound. She inches her bottom up the branch so she is completely hidden by the leaves. Buster's green fur camouflages him well, but she gestures for him to stay still and quiet anyway.

Sure enough, Mrs. Halloway's broomstick comes into view just above them. Polly watches in horror as it hovers above Flora's little house for a while, then drifts downward to land gently on the ground.

Mrs. Halloway props her broomstick against a tree, then walks along the stepping-stone path toward the front door. Polly holds her breath. She takes Buster's paw and feels it shrink a little in her own.

*Oh no, oh no, oh NO!* Polly thinks. *Where in blooming moons is Miss Spinnaker?*

Mrs. Halloway **raps the heavy brass knocker** three times and Flora opens the door. Compared to tall and spindly Mrs. Halloway,

Flora looks like a little pudding in her faded gray smock and yellow cardigan. But before Mrs. Halloway can even open her mouth to speak, Flora has wrapped her arms tightly around her waist in a happy embrace.

"Oh! What a lovely surprise!" Flora calls out loudly in her high, raspy voice. "It's little Deidre Halloway. Iris's old classmate. How lovely to see you!"

Polly can tell Flora is yelling this out as loudly as she can as a warning for them all to hear. She can't see Mrs. Halloway's face, but she sees her thin body stiffen in Flora's arms. Flora pulls back again to look up into Mrs. Halloway's face, her hands still firmly clasping her shoulders.

"Oh, look at you! You haven't changed a bit. Just a little grayer around the temples, but that happens to the best of us," she says, patting her own dyed-pink frizz. "What's taken you so long to come and visit me, dearie? How did you know I was here? You still keep up with Iris, do you?"

Finally Mrs. Halloway opens her mouth to speak, but even though she is trying to sound authoritarian, her voice comes out flustered and awkward after Flora's unexpected flurry of enthusiasm.

"Yes, er, no, I mean, it's Iris who I am looking for, Mrs. Spinnaker," she says. "I saw your son in town and he let me know you live out here now," she says, her voice sounding firmer. "I thought you might know where your daughter is? I have reason to believe she might be hiding a very dangerous monster."

Polly hears Buster gasp and she squeezes his paw tightly, telling him to be quiet. He shrinks a little further.

"Oh no," Flora says, shaking her head convincingly. "Iris doesn't visit me much anymore. I would have no idea what she's up to these days, I'm afraid. But that's children for you, isn't it? Slave after them their whole childhoods and then they grow up and you don't see hide nor hair of them. I do hope you are a better daughter to your mother than my Iris is ..." she rambles.

*What a good liar you are!* Polly thinks. She is amazed at how calm Flora seems.

"And as for monsters," Flora continues, "well, like the rest of us, she doesn't have *anything* to do with them, as far as I know. After all, it wouldn't do to have such a well-respected teacher mixing with **monsters** now, would it?"

"Hmm …" says Mrs. Halloway. But Polly hears by the tone of her voice that she is not completely convinced. "Well, maybe you might like to invite me inside?" she asks, and Polly's heart begins to race. "I've been flying for hours now and I wouldn't mind a cup of tea and to sit down for a while …"

At that moment Flora begins to cough. She bends over, clutching her chest, and

# splutters
## and hacks

all over the place. Mrs. Halloway takes a step backward.

"Oh, sorry," Flora says, standing upright again and wiping her mouth on her sleeve. "I don't know if I'd be coming inside if I were you. You see, I've a terrible case of flackity at the moment."

Flora **squeezes** her eyes tight and for a moment her face becomes as pink as her hair. Then Polly hears a loud noise

# erupt

## from Flora's

## bottom.

Polly has to pinch her lips together to stop herself from giggling and she glares at Buster to remind him not to laugh. It would be a disaster if he began to blow up in size! "Oops! Oh, I do beg your pardon!" Flora says. "Was up all night with it, I was. It's awfully contagious, too. You don't want a case of flackity when you're obviously such a busy witch now, do you, dear?

I wouldn't risk it. But don't worry, if I hear from Iris, I'll be sure to tell her you called by. I'm so happy to hear you two witches are still in touch.

Thank you so much for dropping by, dearie. And do give my regards to your mother."

And with these last words, Flora steps back into the house and pulls the heavy door firmly shut behind her.

Mrs. Halloway hesitates at the door for a moment, then spins around and snatches up her broomstick. Polly catches a glimpse of her **angry red face** as she lifts up from the ground and zooms past them to clear the trees once more.

Only then, when Mrs. Halloway is a black speck against the clear blue sky, can Polly finally breathe normally again.

# Nine

Polly pokes her head out from the leaves, her heart a skittish monkey in her chest.

"Wait here," she instructs Buster, and swings down through the branches. She runs into the house to look for Flora and Mortimer, but they are not in the kitchen. Pausing in the hallway, she hears low voices from the bedroom at the end of the corridor and tiptoes closer to listen.

Flora's voice is too soft to hear through the door, but it is easy to catch snippets of what Mortimer is saying. He is angry and his voice is loud.

"I know it's dangerous for them out there, but they can't stay here!" he growls. "Look how close we came to being discovered. Imagine what those witches would do to you, or me, or even Iris if they found out about us. Do you really think the Committee mothers at the school would be happy to hear their children are being taught by the stepdaughter of a *monster*?

"No!" he continues. "I *won't* calm down. That job means too much to Iris, and you mean too much to me, for us to risk everything by having these two in our house with that evil witch out looking for them. We haven't hidden out here for five years with no contact with any of our friends or families only to have these two youngsters bring trouble to our door ..."

Polly feels her eyes spring with tears. How she wishes she could take back all the trouble she has caused. If only she knew a spell to reverse time and put everything back to how it was before that terrible day at the gallery. Ever since then, it seems she brings trouble with her wherever she goes. And now she has even made trouble for kind, sweet Flora and Mortimer!

She runs back down the corridor toward the living room. There is Miss Spinnaker's blue velvet bag hanging on the chair, waiting for her to return. Polly snatches it up and, as she is about to leave the room, she hesitates for a moment before grabbing Miss Spinnaker's old school spell book and stuffing it into the bag.

Running past the kitchen, she ducks in to grab a handful of ripe pricklefruits and the spickleseed bread wrapped in cloth. She has no idea where she and Buster will go  or how long they will be gone, but she figures it can't hurt to have as many supplies as she can find. Last of all, she plucks a small jar of healing potion from the first aid shelf by the door and tucks it into the bag.

There is a notepad and pencil on the table where she can see Flora has begun a shopping list. Polly rips off a page and scrawls a hasty note:

Thank you so much for having us.
I am sorry to have caused you trouble.
I took some food and potion. I hope that's OK.

Love, P & B.

Then she tucks the notepad and pencil into the bag, too, before heading out the front door to where she knows Buster will be waiting.

Their true adventure starts now.

# Ten

Buster tosses Polly up onto his shoulders and the two of them bound off deep into the forest, before Flora and Mortimer can notice they have gone. Polly knows Mortimer is kind and that he probably didn't mean any of those things he said, but he and Flora never asked to be pulled into this terrible mess.

Polly can't wait around for Miss Spinnaker any longer. She knows where she is meant to be, even if her teacher has forbidden her from going there. She doesn't have a choice. She is a Silver Witch and the stones have told her that this is what she must do. Somehow, she knows there is something in the Hollow Valley Mines that will make things right again. Something to do with her father.

Polly hasn't told Buster about the vision the stones sent her yet. She has been waiting for the right time. For now, all she can think of is to get away from Mrs. Halloway – and fast! For all they know, she may still be flying overhead, scanning the trees, desperate to hunt them down.

Buster runs as fast as he can until they reach the **deepest, darkest** part of the forest. Here the light is dim and the trees are so closely packed together that even the birds no longer swoop through. This is where they will hide for now.

Buster slips Polly off his shoulders and onto the ground. He puts his paws on his knees and leans against a tree trunk to slide down into a squat.

"Do … you … have … any … water?" he pants. His fur is covered in a sheen of sweat.

"Oh!" Polly says. Her brow furrows. She slips the velvet bag off her shoulder and rummages about in it, even though she knows this is the one vital thing she forgot. "I have pricklefruits?" she says, holding out some of the pink, spiky fruit.

Buster takes one of them and peels back the coarse skin with his teeth. He sucks at the juice, but Polly knows it won't be enough to keep them going for long. She burrows into the bag a little deeper. "And, look! I have Miss Spinnaker's wand. And her old spell book, too!" she says, her voice full of hope. "Maybe there is a spell in here to find water?"

She sits on the dirt beside Buster and opens the old exercise book across her knees to read out the list of spells on the front page. As usual, when she tries to read the words, the letters dance across the page. She traces her finger along one line as if to hold it steady, and slowly reads out the words. "Rock mo … ving smell …" she begins.

Buster **snorts with laughter,** spraying pricklefruit everywhere. "Rock moving *smell*!" he hoots. "Ha! That's hilarious! Good one, Polly!"

Polly frowns, snapping the book shut. "It's not funny, Buster!" she says, shoving it onto Buster's lap. "You read it then if you're so clever!"

Buster's face falls. He stares at Polly, who looks away from him, her face scrunched up with hurt. "You can't *read*?" he says, astonished. "But you're so smart!"

Polly realizes this is the first time Buster has seen her try to read something aloud. He has no idea how difficult it is for her. "It's got nothing to do with being smart or not, Buster," she grumbles. "Miss Spinnaker says lots of smart people have trouble with reading." She crosses her arms tightly and kicks at a clod of grass with her heel.

"Polly," says Buster. "I'm sorry! I didn't know you couldn't read."

"I *can* read!" Polly says. Her mouth bunches up tightly as she feels a familiar sting at the corners of her eyes. "I *know* the words. It's just the letters in the books. They trick me. It's like they move around when I'm trying to read them so I read out different words than what's there." Her voice comes out low and small. "That's why I'm so bad at school."

"Does Miss Spinnaker know?" Buster asks. He is feeling Polly's **sadness** and **frustration** so strongly now he has shrunk to almost the same shape and size as her, and his fur is tinged with a helpless shade of blue.

Polly shrugs. "A little bit. I don't know how much. I try and hide it most of the time. But it's getting harder. The witches at school make fun of me when I have to read aloud. They call me **Pumpkin-Head Polly**."

"Well *that's* pretty silly!" Buster snorts. "Why would they think calling someone a pumpkin is a *bad* thing? Pumpkins are *delicious*. They should at least call you something that doesn't taste good. **Like weevils. Or spickleseed.** Spickleseeds are horrible. My mom puts them in bread sometimes. They get in your teeth. Oh, but that doesn't sound the same, does it? Spickleseed Polly doesn't really work." He scrunches up his face as he thinks about it.

Polly giggles. She can never tell if Buster rambles on like this just to make her laugh or if this is what he's really thinking, but it doesn't really matter. Either way, he is the **sweetest, kindest friend** a witch could ever have, and he always knows exactly how to make her feel better.

She puts her arms around his big neck and hugs him tightly until he is back to his normal shape and size again. Then she tucks Miss Spinnaker's book back into the velvet bag and swings it over her shoulder.

"Well, we're not going to find water sitting around here, are we?" she says, standing up and holding out her hand.

When she tugs at Buster's paw, he jumps up into a standing position.

"And she's *strong* too!" he yelps. "Is there nothing this witch can't do?"

Polly laughs. "All right. Enough silliness, Buster. This is a **very serious adventure** we are on!"

Buster makes a serious face and glowers past Polly into the forest behind her. "Anyone out there who makes fun of my Polly or calls her Pumpkin Head or Weevil or Spickleseed or anything mean like that has to deal with *me!*" he growls menacingly.

Then he tromps off ahead and Polly has to skip to keep up with him.

# Eleven

Now that the forest is dense enough for them not to be seen from above, and the immediate danger of Mrs. Halloway has passed, Polly and Buster trundle more slowly through the trees. Polly looks out for slipper weeds because her father once told her that if you suck them they can keep you going until you find water. Buster strides ahead, his monster senses on alert for a river or a stream.

When they were little, Polly's father would often take her and her sister hiking through these woods on the outskirts of town, but she doesn't remember them ever coming as far as this. Here, it is quieter than a forest should be. Only the stripy gizzbugs still **whirr** annoyingly around them, and Polly swats at one every now and then before they can land on her and sting.

Eventually, Polly thinks she spies a bunch of slipper weeds in the hollow of a gannery tree, its wide, fan-shaped leaves quivering in the breeze. She wanders over to look more closely, then hears a rustling in the branches. She looks up – but it is too late! Something leaps out from where it is hidden among the leaves and lands on Polly, pinning her to the ground.

**"Buster!"** she yelps, her heart leaping in her chest.

The face of the creature is so close to hers she can only see its **bared yellow teeth.**

It **hisses** and **spits** and its eyes **flash white and green.**

**"Buster! Help!"** Polly screams again.

Within seconds, Buster is at her side. He plucks the creature from Polly as if it were only a squalling kitten. It claws at his face, and Buster has to turn his head and hold the creature away from him to avoid getting scratched.

Polly sits up to see what has attacked her and suddenly recognizes who it is.

"Maggie!" she cries before Buster tosses the creature into the bushes. "Wait, Buster. Look! It's Maggie!"

Buster plops the snarling monster back down onto the ground and peers at her more closely. His eyes grow wide with joy when he recognizes the monster who lives with his family from time to time. Buster's mother looks after broken monsters and monsters who have no other place to go, and Maggie is the most broken and lonely of them all.

"Maggie!" he says, picking up her scrawny frame again, this time to squeeze her into a ferocious hug. "Maggie! It's me, Buster! And Polly. You remember Polly, don't you?"

He places her down on the ground again, more gently this time, and she looks back and forth between them, her lined face **crumpled** in confusion. Her eyes light up when she recognizes Buster. Polly, however, she seems to be having more trouble remembering – even when Polly holds up her grubby bandaged hand.

Maggie's bite has almost completely healed, thanks to Miss Spinnaker's magic potion, but Polly knows she still has to be wary. Buster's mother has warned her that Maggie can sometimes lash out if she's startled. But Polly knows this is only because Maggie has had a hard life, which has made her not right in the head. Buster's mother has taught her that all monsters need love, even the most unlovable.

"Maggie!" says Buster. "What are you doing here? Did you run away? Where's Mom and Dad? Are they with you?" he asks. "Maybe they are out looking for us?" he says to Polly, hopefully.

Maggie shakes her head. Then she stands up straight and pounds her chest with one scaly claw. Polly notices she is wearing a tight red vest over her old gray dress. On the top left pocket of the vest, just above her heart, there is an **M** embroidered in gold.

"*M?*" asks Buster. "What's that, Maggie? Is that *M* for Maggie? Did Mom make that for you?"

Maggie shakes her head again and **scowls**. She jabs at her chest with a bony finger and jabs at Buster's, too. Then she glares suspiciously at Polly.

"Oh," says Polly quietly. She has understood. "*M* is for *monster*."

Buster chuckles. "Monster? Is that what the *M* is for? But we know you're a monster, Maggie. What are you doing with an *M* on your shirt, wandering around in the woods out here on your own? Are you lost?"

Maggie shakes her head and rocks from side to side, angrily **hissing** and **spitting** at the ground in frustration.

"I don't think so, Buster," Polly says slowly. "I don't think she's alone. I reckon I know what that *M* stands for. It stands for **Monsters Against Witches.** I thought it was just witches ganging up against monsters, but maybe there are monsters out here forming a gang, too?"

Maggie grins proudly and nods her head. Then she snatches Polly's arm and begins to drag her away.

"Maggie, don't be silly!" Buster says gently. "What are you doing? You don't have to drag Polly like that! Are there other monsters here in the woods? Is that where you are taking us?"

Maggie nods fiercely. But she shoos Buster away with one claw.

"What?" Buster says, puzzled. "You don't want me to come?"

Maggie shakes her head. She is trying to look ferocious, but with her missing teeth and pot belly sticking out from under her vest, it's hard to take her too seriously.

Polly turns to Buster. "I think she's trying to *capture* me," she whispers. "That's probably what she's been told to do. We should go with her and talk to the other monsters. Once they know we're on their side I'm sure they'll help us out. They might even know what happened to Miss Spinnaker. She must have flown through the forest at some stage this morning."

"Oh," says Buster, now understanding Maggie's plan – and Polly's, too. He lopes along beside them. "Good work, Maggie! Those other monsters are going to be very pleased with you, aren't they? Capturing a witch in the forest. You don't mind if I come along as well, do you?"

Maggie pauses for a moment, her brow wrinkling as she considers this. Then she shrugs and nods and scurries off through the trees again, pulling Polly along behind her.

# Twelve

$M$aggie drags Polly until they arrive at a clump of tightly packed bushes. She pushes some branches to one side and Polly and Buster gasp to see what a clever hideout the monsters have created.

In a large clearing, four small huts stand in a circle. They are made from twisted tree branches tied together with rope, and each one has a red flag at the top with a gold $M$ sewn onto it. In the middle of the circle is a firepit with logs stationed around it. Two monsters in red vests like Maggie's look up from their place by the fire. They grin as Maggie approaches with her captive.

"Well, look what this old minnie has brought us!" the larger of the two calls out. He is broad and muscly, with rough ginger fur speckled with white spots. One of his horns has snapped off at the base, leaving only a gray stump. The other horn pokes out awkwardly from the other side of his head. When he smiles, Polly sees that his teeth are broken and yellow.

"That minnie might be a scrawny old thing but she makes a good witch hunter, dunt she?" the monster jokes.

He puts down his cracked tin mug and swaggers over toward them. Buster shifts a little closer to Polly's side and she feels the backs of her knees begin to prickle. This monster doesn't look quite as friendly as she had hoped.

"And who else is this you got with you then, Min?" the monster says. "You here to join our gang, my friend?" he asks Buster, looking him up and down. "You're a biggun, aren't you? You'll make a good fighter."

"Actually, her name isn't Min. It's Maggie," Buster says politely. "She lives at our house sometimes when her family can't look after her. I'm Buster and this is Polly." He holds out his paw for the other monster to shake. "And no, I'm not here to join your gang. I actually don't like fighting. My ma always tells me: *paws before claws*."

The monster **sniggers** as he looks at Buster's outstretched paw. "Well, you're a well-brought-up young monster now, aren't you? But there's no need for all those witch manners out here. All those *pleases* and *thank yous* and crossing the road when a witch is heading toward you and sitting at the back of the bus. **Nope,** my frenkin, no more. We're *monsters* out here and we do whatever we like."

He stretches out his big hairy arms proudly and spins around in a circle to show off their full monster hideout. Along with the handmade huts, Polly now notices there are ropes and swings and tires on chains hanging from some of the biggest branches, and lookouts and cabins built right into the trees. To Polly, it almost looks like a playground and, not for the first time, she wishes she had been born a monster. Witches would never think to build a hideout like this!

The big monster **smirks** when he sees how impressed Polly and Buster are. Then he snarls and grabs hold of Polly's arm. Maggie scurries off into the forest again. "So, you are most welcome to join us, my friend," he says to Buster, "but any ol' witch that comes our way, we lock up in the cage until our leader gets back." And with that he snatches up Polly and carries her away with him.

"Hey, wait!" Buster yells, loping after him. "Where are you taking her? Wait! Put her down!"

As she's carried through the trees, Polly sees the other monster leave his place by the fire to follow them. He is smaller, and wiry, with scaly skin and a long, blue tongue like a lizard's.

"I'm OK, Buster," she calls out. She manages to give him a trembling smile, but she can see he doesn't like this turn of events at all. Not one bit!

Even though she is trying not to show it, Polly can't help feeling a *little* nervous around these two mean-looking monsters. None of the monsters she has ever met before look as wild and fierce as this. But Polly figures she and

Buster are probably as safe here as anywhere else. And at least this will give her the time she needs to figure out how they can get to the mines.

Soon, they arrive at a tall metal cage under a tree. In the cage is a wooden stool next to a little rickety table. On the table is a wooden bowl, a tin cup and an earthenware jug. The smaller monster draws a long key from a leather pouch around his waist and wriggles it around in the hole of the rusty padlock. It snaps open and the cage door swings wide. The big monster shoves Polly in. He is just about to swing the door shut when Buster slips in behind her. The big monster roars with laughter.

"Not *you*!" he guffaws. "You don't have to be locked up. You're one of us!"

Buster stands next to Polly in the cage and puts his arm around her. "I stay with Polly!" he declares. "She's my friend."

"Ha!" snorts the big monster. "Whoever heard of a witch being friends with a monster? You hear that, Zeke? This monster says this witch is his *friend*! You ever heard anything so ridiculous?" He roars with laughter.

"Oh, shut up, Domsley, you make my head hurt with all your carrying on!" the small monster says. "Suit yourself!" he snaps at Buster through the bars. "But you're making the wrong choice. It's **Monsters Against Witches** now, buddy. Don't you know? And you're choosing the *wrong* side."

# Thirteen

The skinny monster strides back to the firepit and rolls a log over toward them, plonking it in front of the cage.

"I don't trust a traitor," he hisses through the bars at Buster. "Any funny business and the little witch gets it!" He slices a long, gnarly finger across his skinny throat. "And I'll take *that*, thank you very much!" he says, reaching into the cage and snatching the velvet bag away from Polly. He peers inside. "Aha! Just as I thought."

He draws out Miss Spinnaker's long brass wand from the bag and tries to snap it across his knee, but it won't bend or break so he tosses it into the bushes. Then he pulls out the food Polly has stashed in there and tosses the bag in the same direction as the wand. "You two will stay in there till Carmen gets back, and there'll be no trouble from you. You hear?"

The big monster sits on the log beside the skinny monster and holds out his paw for some food. They share the pickings between them while Buster watches on hungrily.

Buster turns around to where Polly is sitting on the little stool and she hands him a cup of cool water from the jug. He gulps it down, then squats on the dusty ground beside her. "I don't like those two monsters," he grumbles. "I think we should go."

He reaches out to one of the thin metal bars and pushes it hard. It bends a little. Polly can see how easily Buster could break them out of the cage, but her mind is racing with other plans. She dips her fingers into her pocket and feels the **warmth of the stones**. The mines are beckoning her, but she feels there is more she needs to understand about what is going on in the monsters' hideout first.

"Hold on for a little while, Buster," she whispers. "I don't think they'd really hurt us. I think that little one is just bluffing."

"He ate our food!" Buster protests. "That's not bluffing!"

"I want to find out a bit more about who Carmen is and what she's planning to do," Polly explains. "This is pretty serious, Buster. Don't you see? This whole monsters versus witches thing. There could be a full-blown war if we don't find some way to stop this. We need to find out as much as we can to tell Miss Spinnaker. *When* we finally find her!" she adds.

Buster **hurrumphs** and kicks at the dust. "This isn't the kind of adventure I thought we'd be having. Stuck in a cage, starving to death. That's a *boring* adventure. Not a *fun* one!"

"Oh, Buster!" Polly says. "You only had breakfast a couple of hours ago. I'm pretty sure you won't starve to death. And I promise we'll get out of here soon. All right?"

Buster sighs deeply. Polly can see he is working very hard not to show his feelings in case he changes size or color. She knows he hates other monsters seeing how much he feels things in case they tease him about it, and this makes her heart squeeze for her dearest friend. He is the biggest, strongest monster she knows, but she also knows, all too well, how teasing can hurt in ways that nothing else can.

She takes hold of his paw until a little smile creeps back to his face and she can feel him relax again. Then she stands up and wanders over to the front of the cage.

Polly takes a deep breath and tries to sound braver than she feels. She is not sure which monster she should talk to, but decides the bigger one looks less mean. She presses her face up against the bars of the cage. "When is Carmen coming back?" she asks him politely.

"None of your business," the little one snaps without turning around.

Polly tries again. "Is she your leader?"

The big monster turns his head to answer Polly. His lips are pink and shiny with pricklefruit juice. "That's right!" he says proudly. "Carmen is our glorious leader. She is going to lead us into a new future, where monsters will have the power and witches have to do all the dirty work, like working in the factories and mines. Monsters will sit around like fat bortals in mud and you witches and warlocks will work for us for a change." He swings his big hairy arms out wide, then slaps his chest with three fingers pointing down in the sign of an **M** for monsters.

"It's going to be glorious!"

"Stop saying *glorious!*" the little monster snaps. "You sound like an idiot."

The big monster's face crumples. "You are!" he sniffs.

Polly feels anger heating up her chest. "Not all witches and warlocks are like that!" she protests. "My dad worked in the mines, too." She feels her throat bunch up as the next words come out. "He *died* in the mines."

The skinny monster turns his head just a little, and glares at Polly from the corner of his **mean** eyes. "Boo-hoo," he sneers. "Two witches and three warlocks die and the town will never let us forget it. Thirty monsters also died that day, but to you witches it's as if they never existed. Now go back to your corner and stop bothering us with all your chitchat!"

He spits angrily at the dirt, then goes back to picking his teeth with a stick.

# Fourteen

**P**olly sits down on the little stool, her head in her hands. Buster glares at the monsters guarding the cage. "Please let me break us out," he grumbles impatiently. "I really don't like those monsters and I'm *really* hungry."

"No," Polly says, feeling cross and hurt by the mean little monster. "Just be patient, Buster! We need to see who this *glorious* Carmen is so we can warn Miss Spinnaker." Once again she wonders why her teacher didn't come back for them like she said she would.

They sit and they sit, and the sun shifts higher in the sky. Soon, it is shining straight down on them and, even though they are shadowed by the trees, Polly is feeling hot and sticky and dusty. She can see that Buster is feeling hot and hungry too, even though he is trying his hardest not to show it.

The stones *burn* in Polly's pocket, and she knows they are calling her to the mines. There is something there they want her to see, and their call seems to be getting more and more urgent.

But now that she has decided they will stay

and wait for Carmen, that is what they will do. When Polly sets her mind to something, there is very little that will change it. There is also a little part of her that wants to prove to the **mean little monster** that his horrible words didn't affect her. So she will sit there in the blazing sun for as long as it takes.

After some time, they finish the last of the water in the jug. Polly calls out to the monsters to let them know and the big monster unlocks the cage and lumbers in with a wooden barrel over his shoulder. He unplugs a cork and fills their jug with cool, fresh water.

"Sorry about your da," he whispers as he plugs up the heavy barrel again and sets it on the ground. Then he looks up toward the front of the cage briefly before pulling out a crust of bread from his pocket.

"Oh, thank you!" says Polly, surprised by his unexpected kindness.

### Buster's tummy grumbles loudly.

"You have it, Buster," Polly says. "I'm OK."

Buster's eyes widen with excitement, but he quickly catches himself before snatching it out of the big monster's paw. "No," he says firmly. "You must eat half, too, Polly. That's only fair!" And he breaks the little scrap of bread into two tiny morsels for them to share.

Domsley watches on in amazement. He scratches the stump of his broken-off horn.

"Why are you two so nice to each other?" he asks, genuinely baffled.

"We're friends." Polly shrugs, nibbling at her crust of bread to make it last. Buster swallows his in one gulp and watches on hungrily.

Domsley frowns. "But I thought all witches and monsters hated each other?"

"Not *all* of them," Polly says. "That's just silly. Do you even *know* any witches or warlocks?"

Domsley's top lip curls into a sneer. "Sure I do! There's a mean old warlock who runs the factory I work in. If we show up even five minutes late or take a little bit of extra time for lunch he cuts our pay. It's not like we earn a proper wage either! One time my ma was sick and I had to stay home to look after her, and he gave my job to another monster. Worked there for fourteen years I had, and I'm back to sweeping floors again." He spits at the ground. "That's why I left and came here to join Carmen's gang. At least she feeds us proper."

"That warlock sounds **horrible,**" Polly agrees. "But there are good witches and warlocks, too. Just like there are good and bad monsters." She smiles. "And you, sir," she says cheekily, "I can see, are secretly a *good* monster." She taps him on each shoulder as if to knight him. **Domsley grins proudly.** "Him, on the other hand ..." she gestures toward Zeke, who is cleaning out his ear with the stick he had just been using to pick his teeth. "Not so much."

"He's OK," Domsley says, quietly. "Just real angry, is all." He lowers his voice even further. "His da died in that mining accident too, you know. Ever since then he's angry all the time. Eats him up like a **poison,** it does. Sometimes, bad things that happen to you on the outside can make you get bad on the inside, too."

Polly peers over Domsley's shoulder to where Zeke is sitting, staring out into the forest, and suddenly she can see that his eyes are not mean, after all. They are sad. Hollowed out with sadness and anger, and she feels her heart ache a little for this other being in the world who has also lost his dad.

To Polly, there is nothing worse that could happen to anyone, monster *or* witch.

Suddenly she sees they are not so different after all.

# Fifteen

Zeke suddenly stands to attention and does the three-fingered sign of the monster on his chest. "Domsley!" he hisses, and the big monster looks up.

"Oh, leaping lumbears!" he mumbles, quickly snatching up the water barrel and hoisting it back onto his shoulder. "You two stay here!" he says gruffly, and bumbles out of the cage, locking it behind him. Then he stands beside Zeke, his paw held the same way.

"What is it?" Buster asks.

Polly feels her heart begin to flip about like a fish. "It must be Carmen," she whispers, standing up anxiously, then changing her mind and sitting back down.

Through the bars of the cage she sees a small group of monsters lumbering toward them, maybe five or six. They are all different shapes and sizes, and all dressed in the same red vests, except the one in the middle also wears a pair of studded silver cuffs on her wrists.

*That must be Carmen!* Polly thinks, and she feels a ripple of nervousness pass through her.

Carmen is tall and stately, with dark-blue fur flecked with streaks of silver. She has a long, narrow face, and wide, almond-shaped eyes that glitter like emeralds. While the other monsters lumber and jostle about, she seems to glide through them, walking with long, determined strides, as though she always knows exactly where she is going

147

and what she is meant to be doing.

Polly can't help but feel impressed.

Carmen turns to talk to the monsters on either side of her as she walks. One of them steps away, and someone else steps up beside her. It takes a moment for Polly to believe what she is seeing.

*It can't be!* she thinks. *But that's impossible!*

"Miss Spinnaker?" she gasps.

The huddle reaches the cage and Zeke and Domsley step to one side, still doing the three-fingered salute.

"We have captives!" Domsley proclaims proudly to Carmen, whose eyes have widened in horror.

# "Oh, for goodness' sake!"

she growls in a deep, husky voice. "Domsley, Zeke, whatever were you thinking? These are *children*! And what in blooming moons are *you* doing in the cage?" she asks Buster, who scuffs his feet awkwardly beside Polly. "You're a *monster*!" Buster says nothing. There is something about Carmen that makes it hard to find the right words to say. "Let these two out. Immediately!" she commands.

Zeke scowls, but pulls the long key out of his pouch and does what he is told.

Polly and Miss Spinnaker stand staring at each other, their mouths open.

"What are you *doing* here?"
Miss  Spinnaker asks Polly.
"What are *you* doing here?"
Polly shoots back.

Miss Spinnaker's face reddens a little and she frowns. "Polly, Carmen is a very old friend of mine. Just like Buster is a friend of yours. She asked me to go with her to speak with Mayor Redwolf about what has been happening recently with Deidre Halloway, and to see if she can help us calm things down. But you shouldn't be here! It's not safe. I thought I told you to wait for me at my mother's!"

"But you didn't come back!" Polly protests. She can't help feeling a little miffed. Why didn't Miss Spinnaker tell her *this* was what she was planning to do when she left them behind that morning? Polly thought they were in this *together*!

"Mrs. Halloway came looking for us at your mother's house," Polly explains. "We couldn't stay there. She might have come back again. She might have seen *Mortimer*!"

Miss Spinnaker claps her long fingers across her mouth, her bracelets jangling.

Carmen's green eyes glitter angrily as she listens to the conversation. "I know who you are!" she says to Polly, suddenly furious. "You're that witch who made up those stories in the newspaper about monsters being dangerous. *You* started this! And *you're* her friend!" she says to Buster, who shrinks a little in fear. "*You're* the one Deidre Halloway is after!" Carmen draws up to her full size and towers over Polly

152

and Buster. "And you *dare* come into my camp and risk bringing Deidre Halloway and her followers *here*?" she roars.

The monsters around her growl menacingly, and rock from side to side, cracking their knuckles and glaring at Polly and Buster.

Polly feels her bottom lip begin to tremble as she looks up into the monster's furious face. Her tummy curls and her heart begins to race.

"Carmen, stop!" Miss Spinnaker says, and even though her teacher is much smaller than the monsters' fearsome leader, Polly can see she is the only one there who is not the least bit afraid. "Polly made a mistake by doing that spell in the gallery and she is still paying for it. Deidre Halloway is the one who twisted the story around. Polly and Buster are both innocent. Their friendship is a good and beautiful thing. Deidre Halloway knows that if other monsters and witches see that friendships like theirs can exist she will have no way of dividing our town. And so she will do anything to destroy them. They need our protection, Carmen. Can't you see? They are our only hope for a peaceful future."

"It's true," comes a mumbling voice from behind them. Polly turns and is surprised to see Domsley step forward, despite Zeke kicking him in the shin. Domsley's face reddens and he pulls anxiously at his big bottom lip as he talks.

"They're good ones, these two. Done no harm to no one, and they are real kind to each other. He could've left that witch behind and walked free," he says, pointing to Buster, "but he stayed beside her, good and true. I never seen nothing like that before. Warms the heart, it does. Makes me feel hopeful that all monsters and witches can get along just like them someday."

"Rubbish!" Zeke snaps. He pushes Domsley out of the way and sneers into Polly's face. "Once she's grown up she'll be the same as all them other witches and warlocks in Blackmoon Coven. There isn't one I trust. Not even you!" he hisses, pointing at Miss Spinnaker. "Bad to the bone, they all are. Your Mayor is never going to listen to us! Never has and never will! I say we stay true to our original plan." He turns to the other monsters. "What do you think, my friends?" he snarls. "I say the only way we will ever get what we want is to fight!"

"Fight! Fight! Fight!" growl the other monsters, getting louder and louder, until Carmen lifts up a great furred paw to silence them.

"We are a team and we will decide our way forward *together*," she says firmly. Then she pauses. Her ears prick up and she tips her head back to squint up into the bright glare of the sky. Her eyes grow wide and her voice grows harder and steelier. "But for now, it seems we have other, more urgent, problems to solve."

Polly looks up at the sky. In the clearing above the monsters' camp, she sees what Carmen has seen.

A black figure on a broomstick circles above them like a crow.

# Sixteen

"Deidre Halloway!" Miss Spinnaker gasps. "She's tracked you down! You two have to leave, Polly. And fast!"

"I told you that little witch was trouble!" Zeke shrieks, swinging himself up into a tree. "This is all her fault!"

As the first bolt from Deidre's wand shoots from the sky, the monsters duck for cover, hiding in huts and diving into bushes. The bolt cracks into the earth, leaving a long scorch mark across the grass that ends only inches from Polly's feet. She jumps backward in fright. Only Miss Spinnaker and Carmen stand their ground.

"Miss Spinnaker," Polly yells over the commotion. "Your wand is here. In the bushes! I brought it with me."

Miss Spinnaker doesn't take her eyes off the sky for a second. Polly watches her lips flutter and, instantly, the wand soars into her outstretched hand, like a pin to a magnet. She holds it out in front of her just as the next electric-green bolt shoots toward them. Miss

Spinnaker deflects it with her own bolt and it bounces back into the sky.

"Coward!" hisses Carmen, her fists tight against her hips. "Come down here and fight me! Then we'll see who's the strongest!"

"Polly!" Miss Spinnaker says again, even more urgently this time. "Go! Now! My broomstick is by the big morpett tree just outside the clearing. Fly straight home and don't stop. We'll keep Deidre distracted while you escape. Just follow the line of pall trees and they will take you back into town."

"But what about …?" Polly stutters.

**"Polly! Buster! Now!"** Miss Spinnaker yells, just as another bolt comes cracking toward them. Miss Spinnaker is distracted by Polly's dithering and a small bush to her left bursts into flames.

Buster doesn't need to be told twice. He swings Polly up onto his shoulders and gallops out of the clearing.

Polly catches a glimpse of midnight-blue velvet in the bushes. "Miss Spinnaker's bag!" she yells, and Buster snatches it up and tosses it to Polly without missing a beat. They arrive at the big morpett tree and see Miss Spinnaker's old broomstick leaning up against it.

Polly jumps off Buster's back. She picks up the broomstick and turns the long wooden handle around trying to work out how it starts. It is an old-fashioned model, which means there are no buttons or levers and, for a moment, Polly is stumped.

She takes a deep breath to calm herself, then she remembers. Holding the broomstick handle firmly in both hands, she rubs the bristles along the leafy forest floor in firm, brisk strokes.

*Come on, old broomstick!* she begs.

The broomstick sputters and smoke drifts from the bristles, but nothing else happens.

Buster watches on in dismay. "It's not going to start!"

"Yes, it will, Buster. It's just old." She scrapes the bristles against the ground again and again, but nothing happens.

"Try the stones!" Buster yelps.

"What?" says Polly.

"The stones!" Buster repeats. "In your pocket. They're magic, aren't they?"

Polly pulls the pouch out of her pocket and rubs it against the handle.

"Hurry, hurry, hurry!" murmurs Buster.

"I'm doing what I can!" says Polly, her heartbeat in her ears.

"Polly," says Buster, swaying nervously from foot to foot as the noise of the witch battle gets louder and louder. "Maybe we should just run?"

Polly blocks out Buster's nervous chatter. She blocks out the noise of the woods. She focuses only on the stones and imagines them sending their energy deep down into the broomstick handle. Suddenly they burn hot and the broomstick sputters to life.

"Jump on!" Polly yells.

She clambers onto the stick and feels Buster climb on behind her, his arms closing tightly around her waist.

"Oh, Polly," he moans. "I don't like broomsticks. I really don't like them at all!"

"Just hold on!" Polly yells, pulling the tip of the handle toward her. The broomstick judders twice, then soars upward.

The monster's hideout is soon spinning away from them, getting smaller and smaller as they crash through the branches toward the sky.

# Seventeen

Polly and Buster soar higher and higher. The bright-blue leaves of the pall trees are easy to spot among the autumnal reds and golds of the other trees, and Polly can see they create a clear path that leads directly back to town.

They follow the blue streak toward home, just like Miss Spinnaker told them to, but Polly can still hear the cracking of sparks and smell

the burning of grass and bushes. Her heart is a tight ball of shame.

*It's true!* she thinks. *Everywhere I go I cause trouble. That horrible Mrs. Halloway would have never found the monsters' hideout if it wasn't for me! She would never have found dear Flora and Mortimer. If it wasn't for me, this war between witches and monsters wouldn't have started at all!*

The sun stings Polly's eyes and her cheeks burn. She can feel Buster hiding his face in her wind-tangled hair and she knows he will have his eyes squeezed shut, queasy from the speed.

Polly knows Buster would like nothing more than to go home to a hot meal and a warm bath right now. There isn't anything she would like more either, and of course she also wants to see her mother and even her sister again. And she knows she should do what her teacher told her to; after all, Miss Spinnaker is older and wiser and far more powerful than Polly could ever hope to be.

But the stones burn hot in her pocket. Calling her, pulling her, stronger than ever. And she can almost hear her father's voice in her ear. Telling her to be brave. Telling her to listen to her heart.

*I can't just go home!* Polly thinks. *Not when everything is still so messed up out here!*

And without another thought, she turns the broomstick around.

"What are you doing?" Buster yowls. "This isn't the way home!"

"I can't let Mrs. Halloway destroy the monsters' hideout," she yells, her chest filled with an anger that makes her feel **fierce and brave**. "She is after *us*, not them! Somehow, she keeps tracking us down. There must be some way she can sense where we are. How would she know to come looking for us at Flora and Mortimer's house? Or even here, deep in the forest?"

The stones burn hotter and hotter as she flies toward Mrs. Halloway. And suddenly Polly understands. "Of course! It's the stones! Mrs. Halloway can feel the pull of the stones, too, Buster! *That's* how she has been able to track me down."

She thinks about tossing the magic stones into the forest below, far from where Mrs. Halloway is circling, to see if it will draw her away from the monsters' hideout. But then she sees Mrs. Halloway swooping in and out of a thin line of smoke above the treetops, sparks flashing from her wand, and she has an even better idea.

"Mrs. Halloway!" Polly yells, as loudly as she can. "Over here!"

Mrs. Halloway looks up just as a flash from Miss Spinnaker's wand below strikes the end of her broomstick. The bristles burst into flame. Mrs. Halloway chants a spell to put out the fire, but even before Polly has spun her broomstick around again, she can see the Silver 500 has been damaged. It wobbles precariously, its bristles singed and smoking.

"Over here!" Polly yells again, glancing back over her shoulder, as she flies away from Mrs. Halloway, across the treetops and toward the mountains. Even though Mrs. Halloway's broomstick has been hit, Polly knows she will have to fly as fast as she possibly can to avoid being caught.

"Oh, Polly," Buster groans as he holds on tight. "Where are we going?"

"We have to get Mrs. Halloway away from the monsters," Polly shouts. "It's my fault she found them. We have to make her follow us and then I'll find us somewhere to hide."

"But where?" Buster yelps. "You said she will find us anywhere as long as you have those stones in your pocket. Why don't you just get rid of the stones, Polly?"

"I can't!" Polly cries. "Don't you see? Ever since Miss Spinnaker activated them they have been sending me messages, stronger and stronger. There's something they want me to do. Something important. Something that might make everything OK again. They didn't choose you, or Miss Spinnaker, or even my big sister, Winifred, who is much smarter and better at spells than I am. They chose *me*, Buster! I may have messed up a lot of things, but that doesn't mean I can't fix them, too!"

Buster groans and Polly lifts her hand carefully from the broomstick handle to reach for his paw. "But I can take you home first if you want me to," she calls softly into the wind. "You didn't ask to get caught up in all this trouble. I would absolutely understand if you wanted to go home now, Buster. I can do this last bit without you. The stones have chosen me to do this thing, whatever it is. Not you."

Polly feels Buster's paw shrink in her hand and she knows he is afraid. She knows he really, really wants to go home. But all the same, she secretly hopes deep in the bottom of her heart that he will say what she wants him to say. What he always says when Polly needs him most.

"No, Polly," he says, his voice quiet but firm.
**"It's me and you."**

Polly smiles as she answers him.

**"And you and me."**

# **"And that's the way it will always be,"**

they say together, and Polly's heart soars with gratitude.

Because nothing is ever quite so scary with a best friend by your side.

# Eighteen

They skim the treetops and, as the forest falls behind, Polly spies the jagged blue mountain range that is the farthermost point of Blackmoon Coven. An eerie purple mist hovers above it. As they draw closer, Polly smells a terrible smell of damp and jackrock and sorrow.

She stares at the mountain ahead of them. A dark-red gash splits open one side. Even though the sight of it chills her, and Miss Spinnaker's warnings still ring in her ears, she knows this is where she is meant to be. This is where the stones have been leading her ever since Miss Spinnaker activated them in her little kitchen a lifetime ago. That was the moment everything changed.

*Whatever those stones want me to do here,* Polly thinks, *I am not going to let them down. I will prove to Miss Spinnaker that I am not just an ordinary nine-year-old witch, bad at spells and even worse at holding my temper. I am a Silver Witch!*

"Come and get me!" she yells out over her shoulder, to where she imagines Mrs. Halloway will soon be closing in on them. Then she tips the front of the broom gently downward and they begin their descent.

"What *is* this place?" Buster asks, peering over her shoulder, his voice full of fear.

"The Hollow Valley Mines," Polly says quietly. She already knows that Buster will be horrified.

"The Hollow Valley *Mines*?" he repeats. "But those mines are *haunted*, Polly! Everyone knows that! Nobody goes into the Hollow Valley Mines anymore!"

"Well then, we can be pretty sure this is a safe place to hide from Mrs. Halloway, can't we?" she says, sounding braver than she feels.

After all, what witch or monster isn't scared of **ghosts?**

Silently, Polly drifts to the ground. They land on the rocky slope with a gentle thud. Polly hides Miss Spinnaker's broomstick behind a rock and the two of them stand for a moment, staring into the dark gaping hole in front of them.

Polly takes a deep breath. Mrs. Halloway will be only moments away and they have no time to lose. She takes Buster's paw and they walk slowly toward the opening of the mines.

Polly knows she would have never really been brave enough to do this on her own. And, not for the first time, she feels thankful for the warmth of Buster's paw in her hand.

# Nineteen

Polly and Buster step into the long dark tunnel, which slopes down sharply into the belly of the earth. The ceiling drips with dank and the floor is slimy and cold. Daylight disappears quickly once they have walked a little way in, and Polly holds her hands out in front of her, edging slowly forward, hoping she doesn't bump into anything creepy.

"It's dark in here," Buster murmurs, shuffling close behind her. "And spooky. Do we have to go much farther? Can't we just hide here until we know Mrs. Halloway has gone? She won't be able to see us anymore. I mean, I can hardly see *you* anymore! And you're right in front of me!"

"No, I have to keep going farther," Polly says. "I feel like there's something important the stones want me to do here. I don't know what it is, but there's something they want me to find."

"OK," says Buster good-naturedly. "But I hope the stones maybe just want you to find a restaurant or something down here."

"Ha, ha," Polly says, rolling her eyes at Buster's silly joke.

"What would a restaurant in a mine serve?" Buster wonders out loud as he bumbles along behind Polly. "Rock cakes? Crystal shakes? Flipcakes with coal-flavored sauce? Ugh. They wouldn't taste very nice, would they? Would they, Polly?" He chuckles at his own jokes.

Polly ignores him. She wishes Buster would be quiet. She is finding it hard to listen out for danger over his constant chatting. It is getting darker and darker with every step, and Polly feels all her senses on high alert.

"Um, Polly?" Buster says eventually. "How are we going to find what you're looking for if we can't even *see*?"

"I don't know, Buster!" she says. She stops walking, and Buster bumps into her. She feels annoyed with him even though he has done nothing wrong.

She stares into the dark tunnel ahead. It disappears into blackness. *Why didn't I bring a light?* she thinks crossly. *There were plenty of brinkets in the cupboard at Flora's house. I'm so silly not to think to bring a light.*

Polly knows that without a light, they are not going to be able to go much farther. She sighs. But they've come all this way. They can't turn back now!

*Horrible stones!* she thinks. *Why did they bring me here? Why couldn't they have chosen a grown-up, at least? Miss Spinnaker would have been a much better choice.*

But now Polly feels annoyed with Miss Spinnaker, too. She thought her teacher knew everything. But now she knows she's just like all the other grown-ups who pretend they know things when they don't.

Polly feels her **heart hurting**. It aches with **sorrow** and **disappointment**, and suddenly everything that had once seemed so important feels hopeless. Soon, she is so **heavy with sadness** she can barely stand. Her legs give way from under her and she crumples to the floor. Deep, howling sobs clench at her heart and her chest, and squeeze every little glimmer of hope out of her.

"Polly!" says Buster, crouching above her. "Polly!" he calls again, shaking her arms and trying to pull her upright.

"Go away, Buster!" she yells, and her echo yells right back at them. "You are silly and dumb and annoying and I wouldn't even be here if it wasn't for you. I should have never done that spell in the gallery to protect you. This is all your fault!"

This is all your fault!
This is all your fault!
repeats the echo.

"Oh," comes Buster's voice, small and close to her ear, twisted with hurt.

Polly hears him stand up and begin to shuffle his way back to the entrance. Part of her, a big nasty loud roaring part of her, *wants* him to go away. It *wants* to hurt him and hurt him again and again, just to see how much she can.

But then she feels a **tiny flame** burning deep in her belly, just the smallest, bravest flicker of hope struggling against the darkness that is filling her body like a poisonous swamp. This is the part of her that is good and kind and true.

She dips her fingers into her pocket to touch the stones, as she has so often done. They feel warm against her fingertips. But this time their warmth travels up through her hand, along her arm, across her chest and right into her heart, and suddenly her mind begins to clear.

"Wait!" she calls out. She sits up and sees Buster almost at the mouth of the tunnel. He is small and gray with sadness and her heart cracks to know she has done this to him.

"Wait, Buster! It's the mines! It's the mines that are doing this to me. They are pulling me down into their darkness. Can't you feel it too? I'm so sorry, Buster. I didn't mean any of those things I just said to you. You know that. You are the best monster in the whole entire world and there is *no one* I love as much as you."

Buster pauses in the entranceway and turns around. His face is pale with sorrow. "Do you mean it?" he says, his voice small and broken.

"Of course I mean it. Look!" She holds up the pouch of stones. "The stones are making me feel better. And, look, Buster! They are making light, too."

And it's true. When she opens the pouch, the glow from the stones lights up the cave so brightly they can see every jagged detail of the rock face. Polly laughs a hiccupping kind of laugh, tears still drying on her cheeks.

"Come on, my dearest, truest, bestest friend." She stands up and holds out her arms. "Come back, please. I can't do this without you."

She watches Buster's silhouette grow bigger and taller and wider as he walks back toward her.

"I wouldn't have left you anyway," he says when he reaches her, smiling shyly. "I was just pretending. Friends don't leave friends alone in spooky mines."

Polly gives him the biggest hug ever. Then she takes his paw and they face forward again. "All right," says Polly. "Let's find out why the stones want me here, OK?"

"OK," Buster says. "Then can we go home?"

"*Then* we can go home," Polly promises.

# Twenty

Polly and Buster continue down the long narrow tunnel, following the steel railway tracks that stretch endlessly ahead of them. The stones light the way and keep Polly's mind clear from the darkness of the mines.

Buster has stopped talking now, and Polly concentrates hard on listening out for any sounds other than the drip, drip, dripping of water and the echo of their nervous breathing.

On and on they walk, with no idea where they are going and the tunnel growing darker and narrower with each step.

Polly tries to picture what these deserted mines would have been like when they were full of workers. She imagines them noisy with rackety wooden carriages overflowing with rocks and precious stones, hauled to the surface by strong monsters, heaving and panting with effort.

Suddenly Buster grips Polly's hand and pulls her to a stop. "Did you hear that?" he whispers.

Polly cranes her head forward to listen into the dark. She hears a low rushing sound rolling up through the tunnel, like wind singing through the trees or a distant roaring ocean. The hairs on her arms begin to prickle.

"What is it?" Buster whispers again.

"Shhh ..." Polly says, and puts a finger to her lips. The sound comes again, a little louder this time. She grips Buster's paw tightly and she can feel him shrink a little in fear.

Buster jiggles on the spot. "Oh, Polly, oh Polly, oh Polly," he murmurs. "I don't like this. I don't like this at all!"

Polly holds the pouch of stones up high and peers into the darkness. The sound comes again. This time it is louder and clearer and Polly can even make out some words.

"Go away! Go awaaaaaaaay!"

it howls, and Buster pulls hard at Polly's hand.

"Stop it!" Polly whispers to Buster. "Who's there?" she calls out into the dark.

Who's there?
Who's there?
Who's there?
replies the echo.

The voices come again. "We are the ghosts of the Hollow Valley Mines ..." they croon. "Scary, scary ghosts. Run away, little children! Run away!"

"You heard them!" Buster yelps, tugging at Polly's hand, but Polly stands firm. Her heart is pounding and her legs are wobbly, but she takes a deep breath and allows the warmth of the stones to fill her belly with courage.

"Show yourselves!" she demands. "We're not scared of ghosts, are we, Buster?"

Buster stares at Polly like she's gone completely nuts.

Polly widens her eyes at him. "*Are we*, Buster?" she says, firmly.

"Nope!" Buster squeaks. "Nope! Not ghosts. Definitely not scared of ghosts!"

The voice comes again, louder and angrier. "Well, you *should* be! We are *scary* ghosts. *Very* scary ghosts! You should run away while you can! Go home and never come back here again!"

"Why?" shouts Polly, sounding braver than

she feels. "What are you going to do to us?"

There is a pause, and Polly hears an awkward mumbling while the ghosts whisper among themselves. Another spooky voice pipes up. "We are going to scaaaaare you! *That's* what we're going to do!" And as if to prove it, the voice finishes with a long, particularly scary, "HoOO**OOOOO**Ooooo!!!"

Polly frowns. "Well, you'd do a much better job of scaring us if we could see you," she snorts.

The ghosts go quiet. Then, one by one, they slip out from the rocky tunnel walls and hover in front of Polly and Buster. Three shimmering, misty figures shake their ghostly arms at them and make their scariest faces.

But somehow, in the bright light of the magic stones, it is hard for them to seem scary at all. The smallest one is trying so hard to make a scary face it actually makes Polly laugh. Even Buster's tight grip on Polly's hand seems to relax a little.

"OK, not scared," says Polly, and she makes to move past them, pulling Buster along behind her.

The ghosts look at each other in alarm. "NooOO!" they shriek. "You must not go farther! Turn back! Turn back!"

"Or what?" says Polly.

"Or, or …" they look at each other anxiously, "we'll scaaaare you!" They spin around Polly and Buster and shake their ghostly fingers right in Polly's face.

But Polly keeps walking. Up ahead she sees a dark hollow in the side of the tunnel wall. The ghosts notice that she has seen it and spin around her more urgently.

"Go back! Go back!" they shriek.

"This is no place for children. Go home! Run away. Whatever you do, don't go into that cha**aaa**amberrrr!"

Buster shrugs. "Maybe they know what they're talking about?" he says nervously. "That's a pretty spooky-looking chamber."

Polly holds out the magic stones. They are gleaming brighter than ever. "Buster! Don't you understand? There's something in there the ghosts don't want us to see. But look at the stones! Look how brightly they are shining! The stones want me to go into that chamber, so I'm going in! Are you coming with me, or not?"

Buster sways a little from side to side, and chews his bottom lip.

"Buster?" Polly says.

"Of course I'm coming!" he says gruffly. "We're doing this together, aren't we?"

Polly smiles and pushes past the ghosts to step into the chamber.

# Twenty-One

An eerie glow lights up the far wall of the chamber and in the hazy purple light Polly sees the cavernous space is crammed with ghosts. Some of them are playing a strange kind of board game with rocks and gems. Others are chatting, and others float around on their own. The ghosts all look up in astonishment as Polly and Buster step into the chamber. They are monster ghosts, mainly, all different shapes and sizes, but Polly spots a couple of ghostly witches and warlocks, too.

Suddenly, Polly realizes who the ghosts are. These are the ghosts of the miners who were buried here five years ago! Her heart begins to race. Could it be? Is it possible? Is this what the stones have brought her to find? **"Polly!"** comes a familiar voice. "Is that really you?"

She spins around to where the voice has come from, her heart racing. It couldn't be, could it? She can hardly bear to think it. **"Papa?"**

But there he is. It is truly him. His kind, sweet face and dark brown eyes are just as she'd remembered them. **"Papa!"** she cries, and rushes toward his ghostly figure. The other ghosts look on in surprise.

"Polly!" her father cries. "You're here! Oh, my little jamcake. I knew you'd make it eventually!" He holds his ghostly arms out wide and Polly runs into them.

"Papa!" Polly sobs, tears pushing up through her chest and down her cheeks. "It's you!"

Polly sinks into the cool mist of her father's ghostly form. She sobs and sobs as she thinks of all the years she had hoped desperately that she might see him again. And now he is here.

Eventually, she stops crying and her father smiles at her tenderly, his ghostly eyes **shimmering** with tears. "Yes, my darling witchkin. It's me. The stones brought you to me. At last!"

Polly looks up at her father in amazement. "I *thought* that was you calling me!" she says. "I kept seeing you in the visions the stones were sending me. But how did you do it?"

"The *how* is not as important as the *why*, my darling," her father explains, his voice grave and sorrowful. "Blackmoon Coven is in terrible danger. I called you here to help me save it. But we must be quick. Time is running out!"

"Me?" says Polly. "But why? What is happening?"

Her father lowers his sad face closer to Polly's. "Tell me how you felt when you walked into these mines?"

"Oh, awful!" Polly says, remembering. "Sad and angry and hopeless. Like the world was a terrible place." She lowers her voice in shame. "It even made me think horrible things about Buster."

She looks up toward dear, kind Buster,

feeling bad for having hurt him.

He has joined a ghostly

board game and the other

ghosts are thrilled to

finally play with someone

who can move the

pieces with their

fingers, instead

of having to do

it with their minds.

It makes for a

*much* faster

game.

Her father continues. "What you felt was all the $\text{dark}\epsilon\text{st}$ parts of yourself, Polly. The parts you don't necessarily like or feel proud of, but manage to keep buried away."

He sees the embarrassed look on Polly's face and smiles. "It's OK, though, my lovely. Everybody has a dark side. You don't need to feel ashamed."

"Buster didn't," Polly says, frowning. "He stayed the same. He didn't become mean to me, like I was with him."

Polly's father smiles. "There aren't many witches, warlocks or monsters who don't have a mean bone in their body," he tells her. "So I would say Buster is quite an extraordinary monster."

Polly grins and looks over at her friend, who is picking his nose while he considers his next move. She giggles. "Extraordinary, but also occasionally gross."

Her father laughs. Then his face grows serious again. **Very serious.** He runs a ghostly hand across the top of Polly's head and she feels a coolness shiver through her. "That bad feeling you felt, Polly, comes from the gorvan."

"The *gorvan*?" Polly gasps. "Not like the gorvan from witchtales? But I didn't think they were real!"

"I didn't believe in them either, my love," her father sighs. "Even though my monster crew warned me about them. They begged me not to dig our mines too deep into the mountain in case we woke one. But I'm afraid I didn't listen. The lure of the gorvan made me greedy. I became obsessed, digging deeper and deeper, hoping to find the rarest, most precious stones I could. This was a grave mistake, Polly. A very grave mistake." He shudders and looks off into the distance, his eyes sad and heavy.

"Polly, my crew and I have never known such fear in all our lives, and you know as well as anyone I am not a cowardly warlock – and I worked with some of the bravest monsters you could ever know. But even the approaching fog of the gorvan, curling thick and purple up through the cracks of the earth, chilled us to our very bones. Luckily, before the tunnel came crumbling down and took our living bodies with it, and before the gorvan could escape out into the world, I was able to cast one last spell to hold it behind that wall over there. But I'm afraid it won't hold for much longer, Polly. The gorvan is becoming too strong."

Polly looks over at the far wall of the chamber. It glows an **eerie purple** and, as she watches, it seems to **shimmer** and **buckle,** almost as if it were breathing. Her tummy butterflies when she remembers all the spooky tales of gorvans she heard when she was growing up.

"But how is it getting stronger?" Polly says.

"The gorvan **feeds on fear,**" her father explains, "and transforms it into hate. Something must have happened in Blackmoon Coven recently that has begun to feed it. It has been getting stronger every day. That's why I called you here so urgently through the stones, even though I knew it would be dangerous for you to come."

Polly's heart sinks. "My spell!" she says. She never dreamed that the trouble she started on that day could have traveled so far. "Papa, it was my spell that began all this!" And she tells her father all about that day in the gallery and how, ever since then, things have gone from bad to worse.

Her father sighs. "This is not your fault, my

poppet. Fear and hatred have always existed among witches and monsters, and there will always be witches like Deidre Halloway just waiting for any opportunity to stir up the worst in all of us. Your spell may have been the spark, but I suspect even Deidre Halloway would have no idea what has been happening down here in this mine. You see, the more hatred and fear she stirs up, the more powerful the gorvan becomes. And, in turn, the more powerful the gorvan becomes, the more anger, hatred and fear seeps out into the world."

"Oh Papa! But what can we do?" Polly says, her eyes on the oozing purple wall behind him.

"I need you to do the spell to put the gorvan

back to sleep. Only then will Blackmoon Coven be safe," her father explains.

"Why can't *you* just do it?" Polly asks.

Her father smiles. "I can no longer do magic now that I'm a ghost. It has to be you, Polly."

"But I'm *hopeless* at spells!" she stammers.

"You just told me you did a protector spell to save Buster in the gallery," her father reminds her.

Polly shrugs.

"And then again to escape from Deidre Halloway?"

"But it's not like I was even trying to do them," she explains. "They just sort of came out of me. When I *try* to do spells they come out all wrong. Seriously, Papa. I'm worst in my class at school!

I really don't think I'm the right witch to do this. Any other witch would be better than me!"

Polly's father takes both of Polly's little hands in his big ghostly ones. They feel cool and mist like, not like her real father's hands, but his voice is still the same. She looks up into his deep dark eyes, full of love and longing in his pale, shadowy face.

"Polly, you are a *Silver* Witch. I saw it in you when you were born. And it sounds like your teacher can see it, too. Any old witch can go to school and learn to be a Black Witch and do ordinary spells and potions. But you have *true* magic in you. That is something very powerful, and very rare."

"Really?" says Polly in a little voice. She *wants* to believe her father, but it seems too impossible to be true.

"Yes," her father insists. "It's in our family. Your Aunt Hilda was a Silver Witch, too, but she ran away from home before anyone outside of our family could know. So, I'm afraid the responsibility has been passed down to you, like it or not," her father says, smiling at the disbelief in Polly's face. "I wouldn't have left you the magic stones and called you here to do such an important thing if I didn't believe in you. The future of Blackmoon Coven is depending on you, Polly. Now you just have to believe in yourself."

Polly takes a deep breath. All this information

is making her head spin. Up until a few days ago Polly would never have thought there was such a thing as gorvans! Or magic stones or even Silver Witches. Let alone that she'd be meeting her father's ghost after such a long time.

But now that all of these things have come together in one strange moment in a spooky chamber deep underground, she realizes she has no choice but to believe.

"Well, OK," she says nervously. "If you really think I can do it then I'll try. But you'd better tell me *exactly* what I have to do."

"That's my witchkin," her father says proudly, and stands up to call all the other ghosts to attention.

# Twenty-Two

"All right, listen up, crew!" Polly's father says, floating to the top of the chamber so that all the ghosts can see him. "I have great news. My brave Polly has come all this way — with her equally brave friend," he adds, nodding toward Buster, who gives a shy little wave, "to do the spell to put the gorvan back to sleep."

The ghosts all look at each other, their eyes widening in surprise. Then they cheer wildly.

They float around the cavern, slapping each other on the back and hugging each other, tears springing into their shimmery ghostly eyes. "Oh, thank you, Polly!" they call. "Thank you! Thank you!"

"Five long years," one ghost says happily. "Five long years and finally we can move on."

Polly frowns. She looks at her father. "Move on?"

"Yes, Polly," he says. "I vowed to stay here to guard the mines, to make sure the gorvan never escaped, and my faithful mining crew refused to leave my side. For five years we have haunted these mines to make sure no witch, warlock or monster ever came in here. Once you have done the spell to put the gorvan back to sleep, we will no longer be needed. We will be set free."

Polly feels her heart begin to curl up a little inside her chest. She is not sure *this* is what she agreed to. "You mean, if I put the gorvan back to sleep, you are going to go away? Again?"

"Oh, Polly," her father says, understanding what Polly is saying. He takes her to one side, where the ghosts can no longer hear their conversation. "These ghosts have waited five years for this moment, Polly. Imagine. Five long years neither here nor there. It is time, now, for us to move on."

"No!" she says. "You can't!" Fresh tears push up through her chest. "I'll come and visit you," she sobs. "I'll come every day!"

"Polly," her father says, **his eyes shining with tears**. "You have school and your friends and your future. It would not be a life, visiting the ghost of your father in a dark, dangerous mine each day. You would become a ghost yourself. And think of all these other poor souls. This is not just about you and me, my heartkin. You know you must do the spell. Put the gorvan to sleep and save Blackmoon Coven before it's too late. And then *never* come back here again."

Polly looks around at all the other ghosts filling the cavern, watching her with hopeful eyes. She knows her father is right. She can't imagine what it has been like for them all this time, waiting for someone to come and release them. She takes another deep breath.

"All right," she says quietly. "What do I need to do?"

"Thank you, Polly," he says. Then he turns back to his ghostly mining crew. "OK. All of you stand back. Polly is going to do the spell."

"Woohoo!" call some of the monsters, and two of them do a **happy jig.**

Buster looks at Polly and gives her the thumbs-up. "Go, Polly!" he whispers. He smiles at her proudly. Of all the happy, dancing creatures in this deep, dark, gloomy chamber, Buster is the only one who understands how much Polly has missed her father since he's been gone – and how much she has dreamed of seeing him again. He is the only one who truly understands the sacrifice Polly is making by letting him go.

Polly's father turns to her. "You have the stones, don't you?"

Polly nods, wiping her eyes. She holds up the little pouch, damp from the heat of her palm.

"These stones, Polly, come from the very deepest, darkest parts of this mine, from right above the gorvan's heart. That is why they are so powerful," her father explains. "The stones will make sure the spell does what it's supposed to do. Once you've used them here you can take them home with you again, but make sure you keep them somewhere safe. Never let them fall into the hands of someone else. For while they can be used to put the gorvan to sleep, they can also be used to wake it again."

Polly looks down at the little silk pouch in her hand. She has had the stones for as long as she can remember. She knew they were precious, even before Miss Spinnaker activated them, but she would never have dreamed they came from right above a gorvan's heart. Polly promises her father she will guard them with her life and he smiles at her proudly.

"So, what's the spell?" she asks nervously.

Her father smiles. "You know it already, my lovely. I've been teaching it to you your whole life."

"You have?" Polly frowns, confused. "I … I don't know what you mean."

Her father beckons Polly over toward the eerie purple wall. As they approach, she realizes that the strange purple light is in fact a fine mist, **oozing** through the rocks into the chamber.

"The spell is written here," her father says.

She looks where he is pointing and steps in

closer, worried that she won't be able to read it properly. Her father doesn't know how the letters dance around in Polly's mind, and she feels a flutter of panic.

*What if I mess this up?* she worries. *What if I read out the spell wrong and instead of putting the gorvan to sleep I accidentally set it free?* The thought is too terrifying to consider.

But then she smiles. Her father is right. She *does* know this spell. She has known it by heart her whole life.

Carved into the rock face, glowing in the purple mist, are the lines of the poem her father used to say to her each night when he tucked her into bed.

*" Darkling day, drifting light*
*Keep you safe all through the night.*
*Sleep my child, your dreams are sound*
*While the gorvan's underground."*

# Twenty-Three

*P*olly places the three magic stones along the wall the way her father instructs her to. They **gleam brightly** in the gloom.

She looks toward her father, who nods at her to continue. Then she closes her eyes to make her mind go quiet. She feels the ground, steady and solid beneath her.

The words of the spell come into her mind. It is the only spell she knows by heart.

"Wait!" comes a voice from the other side of the cavern.

Polly opens her eyes. She turns around to where the ghosts are watching her from the other side of the cavern, huddled together as far away as possible from the gorvan's wall. One of the ghost monsters is waving at her. Polly looks up at her dad, who shrugs, so she walks over to see what the ghost wants. He clears his throat and pulls at his ghostly beard.

"Um," he says, his voice coming out squeaky and awkward. "I was wondering, I mean if it wouldn't be too much trouble, I was wondering if you wouldn't mind passing a message on to my missus? You see, I never got the chance to tell her that I put some precious stones away for her and the young 'uns. I buried them under the old juniper tree behind the house and I'm feary she'll never find them. I just didn't get the chance to tell her where they was before I … you know."

Polly feels her **heart squeeze.** "Oh, of course," she says. "What's your wife's name?"

"Mrs. Beadle from Dreary Lane," the ghost says. "You'll know her coz she's got this beautiful curly fur; red and yellow, right down to her toes. And the greenest eyes you've ever seen." He sighs, deep with longing. "All six of our littl'uns got them green eyes like their ma. They must be so big. I hopes they're not giving their lovely ma too much trouble. It must be so hard for her now."

"I'd be happy to," Polly says kindly. "I'll go and find her as soon as I get back and pass on your message."

"Thank you, popkin," the ghost breathes. "Your da did always tell us what a good 'un you were."

Polly turns to walk back to the purple wall, but another voice pipes up.

"Oh, er, um – excuse me!" a ghostly monster says, stepping forward and wringing his hands. "Do you thinks you could pass a message on for me as well? I never got the chance to tell my sister I'm sorry for calling her a grumpling old cesspit."

He turns his shadowy face toward the others. "We had an argument the night before – you know, before we got trapped in here. She *is* a grumpling old cesspit most of the time, but I *do* love her. I'd hate her to think that even though we fought like catch and corn, I didn't *love* her. I've been worrying about this a lot these last five years. Polly poppet, can you tell her that for me, dear, do you thinks?"

Polly nods. Then another voice comes. Not the voice of a monster, but a warlock. Polly turns toward it in surprise. "I think you know my niece, Polly," the voice says, and Polly wanders over to look at his face more closely.

"I'm Malorie's uncle," he says. "Mrs. Halloway's brother."

# Polly gasps.

The ghostly warlock nods. "I am so sorry to hear how angry and vengeful my sister has become," he sighs. "Please tell her not to be afraid of monsters. Tell her I loved working with these brave souls every day of my working life. Tell her that monsters are some of the best, most decent creatures I have ever had the fortune to know, and that it was an honor to work alongside them."

His voice drops, and Polly draws closer to

hear what he has to say. "It's not really for me to tell, but she had a bad experience with a monster once," he tells Polly quietly. "When she was young. You'll learn this, Polly. That the most angry people are usually driven by fear. Please try not to judge her too harshly."

Polly opens her mouth to answer, but a chorus of ghostly voices interrupts her.

# "Me too! Me too!"

they call. "Please can you pass on a message to my loved ones, dear Polly?"

Polly laughs. "Of course! Of course! I can pass on all of your messages. But how will

I remember them all, and remember where to take them? Buster," she says, "will you help me?"

Buster raises his eyebrows and winces. "Oh, you know me, Polly," he apologizes. "I have a terrible memory. I can barely remember how many toes I have on each paw most of the time. But don't you have a notepad and pencil in Miss Spinnaker's bag? I saw it in there when I was looking for pricklefruits."

"Oh, of course!" Polly says, looking down at the satchel that's still slung across her back. Deep in the front pocket is Flora's notebook and pen. She pulls them out. "What would I do without you?" she asks Buster and kisses him on the forehead.

Pink **blooms across** his smooth green cheeks.

One by one, Polly travels from one ghost to another, and writes down messages for their loved ones. She decides she is not going to worry about spelling mistakes or messy writing. She knows, this time, it won't matter. What matters is the messages of love, instructions and dedications, and all the other important things the ghosts have thought about over the five long years they have stood guard in this cave.

She **carefully** tears each note from the little notepad, folds it in half and tucks it safely into Miss Spinnaker's soft velvet bag.

Soon, she has a bag full of precious notes and memories rustling against her side.

Finally, she reaches her father. She stands in front of him attentively, the last piece of paper from the notepad in her hand, her pencil poised and ready. This one she will write out as neatly as she can.

"Papa?" she asks. "Is there something you want me to tell Mama or Winifred?"

"Oh," he says, his voice catching.

They stand there silently for a while and Polly feels tears begin to stream down her cheeks. "There are too many words crowding my heart for that one little bit of paper, Polly," he says, his voice full of sorrow. He pauses. "Just tell your mom and your big sister I love them. I never told them that enough when I was alive."

Polly nods and tucks the notepad back into her pocket. She will have no trouble remembering that one.

And now it is time.

Polly pushes all the little paper fragments of love deep into Miss Spinnaker's velvet bag, then goes to stand in front of the wall again. Her **heart is swollen** and her cheeks feel **tight with tears.** She looks into her father's eyes for what she knows will be the last time.

"**Goodbye, Papa,**" she whispers.

"**Goodbye, my treasure,**" he whispers back. "You are a good witchkin and you are doing a good and brave thing. When you have finished, I will be gone. But never forget I will always be in your heart. And you, my darling, will always be in mine."

# Twenty-Four

Polly steps into position again, her feet facing the three bright stones. She closes her eyes and begins to recite the spell. Her heartbeat slows and she feels her feet become as solid as the rock beneath her. Warmth travels through her toes, up her legs, into her chest and along her arms. Finally it reaches her fingertips and they begin to crackle and fizz. Suddenly, a **rush of heat flashes** through her body and her arms fly upward.

**Sparks fly** out of her fingertips, lighting up the chamber, and a gentle hissing sound **slices through the air.**

Polly opens her eyes. All around her are the sighs and moans of the ghosts as they drift upward like pale gray mist, and soon the cavern is quiet. She looks at the gorvan's wall. The purple fog is clearing. Soon, the rock face is as clear as the other three walls of the chamber and she knows the spell has worked. From deep below the ground she hears a gentle rumbling. The gorvan is asleep.

Polly turns to the spot where her father had hovered and sighs deeply. She misses him as much as she ever did, maybe even more, but the pain in her heart doesn't feel like a useless pain now that she has had the chance to say goodbye.

She pictures the faces of the monsters and witches receiving messages from their ghostly loved ones, gone, but never forgotten. She can only imagine what **happy sadness** they will feel.

Now that the gorvan sleeps again, Polly hopes that Blackmoon Coven will return to the quiet, peaceful town it once was.

*And, who knows?* she wonders, feeling unexpectedly hopeful now that the **wooziness** of the spell and the darkness of the gorvan have begun to lift, *Maybe there might even come a time when no one bats an eye at a witch and a monster being friends?*

Polly turns to look at Buster. Her oldest,

dearest friend. They are the only two left in this quiet gloom. He is sitting with his back against a rock wall and his tummy is **rumbling loudly.**

"Are you OK?" he asks Polly kindly, standing up and brushing dust off his bottom. "That was a pretty big spell you did just now, wasn't it?"

"It was," says Polly, smiling. She nods her head up and down slowly to see if she still feels a little **dizzy.** "You know what?" she says, patting her arms. "I actually don't feel too bad."

"Great!" Buster says. "Maybe you are getting better at them?"

"Maybe," says Polly. "Don't tell Miss Spinnaker though, will you? Three spells out of school grounds means I could be expelled from Miss Madden's."

"I won't," Buster promises. And he draws a finger across his lips to show they are sealed. "So, do you think that might be all you need to do here?"

"I think so," Polly says.

**"Yay!"** Buster says happily. "That means we can go home then, right?"

"Right," says Polly.

**"Oh, thank moonbeams!"** says Buster, eagerly leading the way. "I'm starving!"

"Me too," says Polly. And it's true. It feels like years since they ate Mortimer's flipcakes with

Flora's sparkle syrup for breakfast.

Polly picks up the stones from the ground, one by one, and drops them back into the little silk pouch. Their light is growing dimmer and they have begun to cool. And even though Polly is hungry and sad and bone-achingly tired, she knows she has done a good thing.

Her father would be proud of her.

# Twenty-Five

*B*uster takes Polly's hand and swings it in his paw. They have been walking a long, long way up the steep slope of the dark, gloomy tunnel, feeling their way back along the walls in the fading light of the stones. Polly feels sure the entrance can't be far off now, and she can feel Buster's pace quickening.

"What's the first thing you're going to do when you get home?" Buster asks her.

"Have a hot bath," says Polly. She has begun to shiver from the cold. "Actually, no. Hug my mom, *then* have a hot bath."

"I'm going to hug my mom, then eat a whole plate of jamcakes," Buster says. "Hot ones with extra dibblecream on top."

"*Then* have a bath?" Polly giggles.

"Why?" says Buster. "Do I smell?"

"Only like a monster who hasn't washed in two days. And slept in his clothes."

"That's not a bad smell, is it?" Buster asks, lifting up a hairy arm and smelling underneath it.

"No!" says Polly, giggling. "I *love* the smell of dirty monster."

Buster elbows Polly. She tumbles against the wall.

"Hey! Don't you think it's hard enough walking in the dark without you knocking me over?" She laughs and walks a little farther. Suddenly she stops and Buster bumps into her. "Look, Buster! Up ahead. Is that light?" She squints into the darkness. "Do you think it's the entrance?"

Buster pauses to squint, too. "Maybe?" he says hopefully.

"Wait!" says Polly, frowning and pulling Buster close. "Can you hear that?" She gets a familiar funny feeling in her tummy, and the stones begin to grow warm in her hand again. "Hello? Is someone there?" Polly calls out.

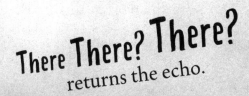

There There? There? returns the echo.

"It better not be *ghosts* again!" Buster mumbles, rolling his eyes.

But before Polly has the chance to answer, a blinding flash of turquoise lights up the tunnel. Polly and Buster are thrown backward onto the hard rocky ground. There is an ear-splitting crack and the tunnel rumbles around them. Buster dashes to cover Polly just as an avalanche of rocks falls down on them from the crumbling walls. He pushes away as many as he can, but they are falling thick and fast.

Again and again the rocks smash against Buster's broad furry back, but he uses all his strength to keep them from hitting Polly. The noise in the tunnel is deafening.

Eventually the cascade slows until only dust and pebbles settle on the pile of rubble. Buster carefully pushes the many heavy rocks away.

"Ow!" he says, dusting off his fur.

Polly sits up, blinking and dust covered. She has a graze on her cheek, but nothing like the big welts Buster has across his back.

"Buster!" she coughs. "Are you OK?"

Her heart begins to race. She sniffs the air in case the avalanche has woken the gorvan, but there is no sign or smell of it. She breathes out in relief. The gorvan must be far enough and deep enough underground for it not to have been disturbed.

"I'm OK," Buster says gruffly, but Polly can see him wince when he tries to stand.

Polly checks all her limbs. She is in one piece. "Mangy mushrooms!" she says. "I would have been crushed if it wasn't for you, Buster. What *was* that? An earthquake?"

Buster shakes his head and frowns. "I don't think so," he says, pointing to something behind Polly. "In fact, I'd say it was more of a *witch*quake."

Polly gasps and scrambles to stand up. She looks to where Buster is pointing. A little distance away from all the debris, lying on the tunnel floor, is Malorie – Mrs. Halloway's daughter. Her foot is trapped under a rock and she cries out in pain.

"Malorie Halloway!" Polly says furiously. "That was *you*? I can't believe it! You did a spell to make those rocks fall! Why would you *do* such a thing?"

Malorie begins to cry. "My mother sent me in here. The spell wasn't meant to hurt you, I promise. Just block you in here."

Polly sees Mrs. Halloway's fancy wand, crushed and broken under the rocks beside Malorie. "And then what?" she shouts. "We'd be trapped in here and left to *die*?"

Malorie begins to cry harder. "I didn't know you'd be in here, too, Polly. My mother told me it was just Buster. And she told me he's a dangerous monster who would hurt me and lots of other witches too, and that I was doing the right thing. That's what she told me, Polly!"

# "You KNOW that's not true, Malorie!"

Polly yells, even louder

than before.

She can feel the rage **steaming up** through her chest and takes some gulps of the dusty air to try and calm down. "You *know* Buster is my friend. That he's always been my friend. Why would I be friends with a monster who is *dangerous*?"

Malorie sobs and sobs. "I'm sorry, Polly! I really am. Oh, please help me. I can't move and my leg is *really* hurting!"

Buster squirms beside Polly in discomfort. She knows he hates seeing anyone upset or in pain and she can feel him shifting anxiously from one foot to another.

"Sorry?" spits Polly, furiously. "*Sorry?* I think it's a bit late for that!"

"You don't know what it's like living with my mother," Malorie cries. "I didn't have a choice."

"Of *course* you had a choice!" Polly hisses. "You *always* have a choice. And you chose to do the *wrong thing,* Malorie. And so for that we are going to leave you here. If your precious mother loves you so much then *she* can come in here and rescue you. But think about it, Malorie. Don't you think it's a little odd she sent her *daughter* into these dangerous, scary mines rather than going in herself?"

Polly pulls Buster's paw for him to follow her as she clambers over the rocks toward the entrance. "Don't worry, Malorie. We'll tell your mother where you are. On our way *out!*"

As they stumble closer, Polly can see Malorie's face is **bleached white** with pain. Her eyes are squeezed shut and Polly almost feels sorry for her, but then she allows her anger to fill her again. Deidre Halloway and her daughter need to be taught a lesson once and for all, she decides, and pulls at Buster's paw.

But he won't come.

"Buster," she hisses. "Come *on!*"

Buster rocks **anxiously** from side to side. "We can't just leave her here," he murmurs, his face twisting with concern.

"Yes. We. Can!" Polly insists, jerking at Buster's paw. "She wanted to *hurt* you, Buster. Maybe even *kill* you!"

But he won't budge.

"*Polly!*" he says, so firmly that she drops his paw in surprise. She has *never* heard him raise his voice before. "You are my bestest best friend in the whole wide world and probably the cleverest and bravest witch I know. I would usually do *anything* you ask me. But not this. Just because Malorie did the wrong thing, doesn't mean we should, too. We are not bad, Polly. We are *good*. Remember?" Polly sighs deeply and slumps forward. She feels tired and achy and dirty and she just wants to be home. But she knows Buster is right. There is no other heart she knows that is as good and true. And she knows there are times when she has done the wrong thing herself, and hurt others without meaning to. She is no different, really, from Malorie.

"All *right*!" she grumbles angrily. "You can lift the rock off her foot then. But that's *all*! She has to walk back by herself. You are *not* to carry her, all right? Even if she *is* hurt!"

But it turns out Malorie can barely stand, let alone walk, so dear, sweet Buster hauls her up over his bruised shoulders and they limp slowly back toward the pale, gray light, each step taking them closer to home.

# Twenty-Six

"He has my daughter! The monster has my daughter!"

This is the first thing they hear, even before their eyes adjust to the light. Polly's heart begins to pound. She would know that horrible voice anywhere.

"Look, look, right there! The monster has my daughter!"

Polly looks up to see a swarm of witches advancing toward them up the steep slope of the mountain. Leading the pack, as Polly knew she would be, is Mrs. Halloway, her snarling face more **terrifying** than ever.

Polly looks toward Buster and sees how the scene might look to the advancing witches. Malorie is slung over his back, clearly hurt, and Buster is loping clumsily toward them, his face twisted with exhaustion.

"That monster has my daughter!" Mrs. Halloway screams again. "I *told* you monsters were dangerous and you wouldn't believe me. And now look what's happened! He's hurt her! Look! The monster's hurt my *daughter*!"

For a moment, Polly sees a look of genuine concern come over Mrs. Halloway's face, as if she has always known that Buster could never *really* hurt a witch, and is surprised to see that this time, perhaps he has.

This, more than anything, makes Polly **seethe with rage**. How dare that horrible, scheming witch blame Buster! How dare she attack him and chase him and spread lies about her dearest friend! Polly decides she doesn't care anymore if she is expelled from school for doing spells. She doesn't care if what she is doing is right or wrong or somewhere in between. She won't listen to Mrs. Halloway attack Buster for one more minute.

Her chest fills with heat and she draws her arms up into the air. But before the hot wind fills her, Malorie's voice rings out, loud and clear.

"**Stop! Ma!**" she calls out. "Stop, everyone! You've got it all wrong."

Deidre Halloway continues to run toward them, but the other witches slow for a moment to hear what Malorie has to say.

"Ma! Stop!" Malorie calls out, louder this time. Her mother reaches them and tries to pull her daughter off Buster's back. Buster shrinks away from her.

"Get off her!" Deidre shrieks. "Let go of my daughter!" She turns to the other witches to seek assistance.

They are hovering uncertainly, unsure of what is really going on and why they were called so urgently to the mouth of the mine, when at this time of night they would normally be at home cooking dinner and preparing their children for bed. In the pink, fading light of the day, Buster looks so exhausted and pitiful it's hard to see how he could seem frightening to anyone.

"Help me!" Deidre Halloway hollers again. "Prisquet! Bordree! Strike him down! Do *none* of you have your wands on you?! Can't you see the monster has my daughter?"

"Ma, stop it!" Malorie says, angrily now. She slides off Buster's back and winces as her injured foot touches the ground. "That's enough!"

Then she looks over her mother's shoulder, eyes blazing, toward the approaching witches, who are muttering among themselves. Many of them have children at Polly and Malorie's school. Polly recognizes the mother of one of Malorie's friends, Willow Leafly, in the huddle.

"Aren't you ashamed?" Malorie yells. "All of you! Look at him! Does this look like a monster who would hurt anyone?"

Buster shrugs uncomfortably and gives the witches an awkward wave. His fur is matted and his back is bruised, but the kindness of his heart still shines out of him.

"Buster has never done anything bad to me," Malorie continues, despite the terrifying look of rage spreading over her mother's face. "Or anyone!" She turns away from her mother and her voice stays steady and true.

Polly feels a **surge of awe** watching Malorie stand up to her mother like this. She has faced wild monsters, nasty witches and even scary ghosts over the last few days, but in truth, Polly couldn't imagine anything in the world as frightening as standing up to your own mother. She feels a newfound respect for her classmate, who had been almost her friend until the whole **Witches Against Monsters** thing had gotten so out of hand.

Malorie limps slowly toward the gaggle of witches, her face crimson with fury. "It's not the *monsters* you have to be afraid of," she yells at them. "Can't you see? It's my *mother*. My mother is the only bad one here!"

All the witches gasp. Even though they heard these exact same words from Polly only the night before, somehow hearing them from Deidre Halloway's own daughter makes the witches finally stop and truly listen.

"Malorie!" Deidre snaps. "That's enough!" She turns to the other mothers, her voice twisted with embarrassment. "My daughter is obviously not well. She must have hurt her head when she was in the mine. Or … or …" Polly sees her searching desperately for something to convince them. "Polly did a spell on her! That's what happened. That monster-loving witch **brainwashed** my daughter!" She steps forward to pull her daughter toward her, but Malorie hops away and Buster steps protectively in front of her.

"Get away!" Mrs. Halloway shrieks. "How dare you filthy monster come between me and my daughter. Get away this very minute!"

Mrs. Leafly steps forward and grabs Deidre's arm, holding it firmly to keep her from lashing out at Buster.

"Let her speak, Deidre," she says firmly. Mrs. Halloway rises up **ferociously,** but Willow's mother stares her down. "Go ahead, Malorie," Mrs. Leafly says, letting go of Deidre's arm and crouching down to face the small, trembling witch. "Tell us what happened in that tunnel. How did you get hurt?"

Malorie takes a deep breath and turns toward her school friend's mother. "My mother sent me in there. She was too afraid to go in herself! She gave me her wand and told me to go into the tunnel and do a spell to trap Buster because she said he is dangerous. But it's Just. Not. True," she says, her face crumpling.

Mrs. Leafly puts her arm around Malorie.

"Buster should have left me in there, but instead he *saved* me!" Malorie says. "He carried me out on his own back. Buster has never hurt anyone." Malorie begins to sob. "Polly is right. My mother made it all up. All of it. Even the stuff in the newspapers and what happened in the gallery. I should never have listened to her."

The witches' eyes widen and their mouths drop open in shock.

"She's lying!" Mrs. Halloway screeches. "The nasty little grommet is lying. It's that horrible Polly who's put her up to this, I'll bet." She grabs Malorie's arm and tries to pull her away.

"No!" says Malorie firmly. "I'm not coming with you."

"Don't be ridiculous," says Mrs. Halloway, pulling even harder. "You're my daughter. You'll do as I tell you."

"Deidre Halloway!" comes a voice from among the trees. "That's enough!"

Polly looks up in shock to see Miss Spinnaker step out of the dark forest, broomstick in hand.

Her cheeks are flushed and her hair is wild and curly from the ride. She glares at the huddle of witches around the mouth of the mine, shuffling uncomfortably among themselves, embarrassed to be caught up in such a terrible situation.

Then, to Polly's utter surprise, another witch walks out of the trees to stand beside Miss Spinnaker. Polly gasps when she recognizes who it is. She has never met this witch before, only seen her portrait in the hallway at school, but she knows instantly who Miss Spinnaker has brought with her.

Not for the first time, Polly is filled with love and admiration for her clever teacher, who always knows what to do and just the right way to do it. For, standing beside Miss Spinnaker, a look of calm fury on her face, is Blackmoon Coven's very own Mayor Redwolf.

# Twenty-Seven

"Deidre Halloway," the Mayor says in her deep, rumbling voice. She is tall, broad shouldered and dark skinned, with raven-black hair twisted down her back in a long, snakelike plait. She stares at each and every one of them with her glittering, black-rimmed eyes, and Polly sees the mothers from her school all shrink under her glare. When she walks toward them, her black velvet cape swishes around her silver-buckled boots.

"I am **horrified** to think that such an upstanding member of our community would behave in such an **appalling** way," she continues, her voice even lower and angrier than before. "Miss Spinnaker had warned me that this kind of divisive behavior was going on in Blackmoon Coven, but I must say I would never have believed it had I not just witnessed everything that has happened here this evening. This is not the kind of behavior we tolerate here in our little town, Mrs. Halloway. I'm afraid I have no choice but to ask you to step down as head of the Committee."

Deidre Halloway's mouth drops open in horror. "You can do no such thing!" she shrieks. "My great-great-grandfather founded this town. This town wouldn't even *exist* without my family!" Her face **burns red with rage**. "And anyway, I was *voted* in. The Committee has nothing to do with you, Mayor Redwolf. Only the Committee members can vote me out again." She glowers at all the other witches, but they all look away or down at the ground.

Mrs. Leafly eventually clears her throat to speak. "I'm afraid I have to agree with the Mayor," she says, sounding nervous at first, but then becoming more confident as she notices the other Committee witches agreeing with her. "We can't have someone who would risk her own daughter's life as head of our Committee. What would we say to our children? Therefore, I, Daisy Leafly, treasurer of the Committee, vote for you to step down."

"Me too," murmurs another witch, angrily.

"Me too," says another, then another.

Mrs. Halloway stares disbelievingly at them, her face growing more and more crimson and her eyes **dark with hatred.**

# "You will be sorry,"

she screeches. "You will all be **very sorry.**
This war between witches and monsters is
not over yet. You have no idea what danger
I have seen brewing in the woods out there.
And I assure you, every single one of you here
will regret you ever listened to these monster
lovers over me."

Then, seeing that no one from the Committee
will even look her in the eye, she whips her cape
tightly around her, snatches her broomstick

from where it is lying and disappears into the swirling night.

"Good riddance!" snaps one witch.

"What a terrible thing to have done," adds another.

"To her own daughter!" spits a third.

They become **louder** and **braver** now that Mrs. Halloway is no longer around to hear them, and Polly can't help hoping that now she is gone, Blackmoon Coven will return once again to its peaceful ways. Even if she knows herself that what Mrs. Halloway says about the monster army is true.

The Mayor puts up a hand to silence the angry witches. Then she turns back to the three children huddled by the mouth of the mine, all of them desperately in need of a hot meal and a warm bath.

"Buster, I would like to be the first to congratulate you on being such a strong and brave monster, and thank you for saving these two young witches from this dangerous mine," the Mayor declares.

She holds out her hand to shake his paw. "I am not going to ask *how* or *why* you are here in the first place, as you know the Hollow Valley Mines was declared out-of-bounds long ago. I will leave that matter for your parents to deal with as they see fit. But I *will* say that this evening you have proven to be a true hero." She smiles.

"And our town definitely needs more of those. You can be sure that you will receive a hero's ceremony when I can arrange it and, in recognition of your integrity and courage, I would like to award you with the Mayor's medal of honor."

**Polly gasps.** The other witches do, too. No monster in Blackmoon Coven has ever received a **Mayor's medal!**

Polly looks up at her teacher. Miss Spinnaker is smiling at them warmly as if she is the only one there who is not surprised by this news.

Polly smiles back at her. She is sure her teacher had something to do with this unexpected turn of events.

There is a gentle stirring as all the witches gathered by the mine begin to murmur their approval. They nod their heads and step up to Buster one by one to shake his paw.

# "A hero! A hero!"

they chant loudly, hoping that their enthusiasm might make up for their horrible doubts about Buster only moments before.

"But it's not just me …" Buster stammers, opening his eyes wide at Polly, wondering if he is allowed to tell of her bravery in the mines.

But Polly lightly brushes a finger over her lips to remind him of their secret and gestures toward her teacher. She has already decided that for now she will tell Miss Spinnaker it was Mrs. Halloway who chased them into the mines and not her father's ghost who called her there. And she definitely can't tell Miss Spinnaker about the spell her father asked her to do. Disobeying her teacher and doing spells out of school grounds could only result in one thing. And Polly knows she is already going to be in enough trouble with her mother without being expelled from Miss Madden's, too!

She takes Buster's paw and whispers in his ear. "Anyway, it's true. You *are* a hero! Blackmoon

Coven's first monster hero! Can you imagine? But even more than that, you're my very *best* friend. I could have never done any of this without you."

Polly watches Buster **blush** and fill with joy. In no time at all he has grown **so big and full of happiness** Polly has to hold onto his paw tightly in case he floats away.

"Well, I think these three best be getting back to their families before their parents are even *more* worried about them," Miss Spinnaker says, giving Polly a look that lets her know she has some serious explaining to do.

"But where will I go?" Malorie whimpers, and suddenly, after being so fierce and brave, she bursts into tears again from the terrible shock of it all.

"You'll come back with me, darling," Mrs. Leafly says, hurrying over and putting her arm around the small, sobbing witch. "And you can stay as long as you need to. Willow will be thrilled to have the company."

"And I will take you two back home," Miss Spinnaker says. "Do you still have my broomstick, Polly? This rental will be due back any moment now." And, sure enough, as they watch, the snazzy metal broomstick in Miss Spinnaker's hand suddenly beeps three times, then shoots up into the air to make its own way back to Blackmoon Coven's Broomstick Rental Parlor.

Polly nods and points over toward the trees, where she has hidden Miss Spinnaker's trusty old wooden one.

"Oh," says Buster, his happiness suddenly **deflating** from him like air from a balloon. "I have to get on a broomstick again, don't I?"

Mayor Redwolf looks toward Miss Spinnaker, who smiles and nods. Then the mayor turns to Buster. "Well, I thought this time you might like a lift back with me?"

She points down the hill to where her shiny gold Buckmeister is parked. Buster's mouth drops open at the sight of its sleek gold fins and glossy black wheels.

The Mayor chuckles. "I'm not a big fan of broomsticks either," she tells Buster. "Four wheels on the ground has always been my transportation of choice."

# Buster whoops with excitement.

"What about you, Polly?" Miss Spinnaker says. "Do you want to ride in the Mayor's fancy new car, too?"

Polly shrugs. "Nah. I'll come with you, if that's OK?" she says.

Miss Spinnaker smiles. "Of course. And I may even let you steer if you're good," she says, winking.

Soon, the witches are on their broomsticks and Buster is in the passenger seat of the Mayor's car, his grinning face out the window, his fur whistling in the breeze.

# What Happens Next

The sun has set and the sky is a dark velvety blue. One by one, the lights of Blackmoon Coven begin to twinkle, as witches, warlocks and monsters begin to gather their children for dinner and bed.

Only one Black Witch still hovers around the mine, and when it has grown dark and quiet again, she creeps out from where she has been hiding in the trees.

Deidre Halloway looks all around her to check she is alone, then pulls out a small pouch of stones from her pocket. Their gentle glow lights up the night. Holding them out in front of her, she walks slowly toward the entrance of the mine.

Deep down below the crumbling red earth, a creature gently rumbles.

# Acknowledgements

Monster-sized thanks to all my early readers: Cassandra Austin, Davina Bell, Kristen from Squishy Minnie and especially the wonderful L-J and Lija from Three, Four Knock on the Door, who gave me that final boost of confidence to send this next book out into the world.

Without the invaluable support of Marisa, Penny and Luna this story would still be floating around in my head somewhere and I am so grateful to everyone at Hardie Grant Egmont for all their hard work, as well as our amazing designer, Stephanie Spartels, who makes magic happen every time.

I also want to thank all the wonderful children's booksellers I meet while travelling around this country. We would be nowhere without you. I wish I had the space to name you all but will start by giving a special shout out to Leesa at the Little Bookroom, who genuinely makes the world a better place.

Lastly, my biggest thanks go to all my readers. Yes, YOU, right now, reading this book. YOU are who I write for and who inspire me to sit at my desk each day wrestling with stories that won't behave themselves and daring me to venture into those dark places. This book, more than any other I have written, is for you.

# About Sally Rippin

Sally Rippin is the sort of grown-up who remembers exactly what it was like to be a kid. That's one of the reasons her books are so beloved around the world. She has written more than sixty books for children, including the best-selling *Billie B. Brown* and *Hey Jack!* series. Sally's books have sold over four million copies internationally, which is enough to make any monster puff up with happiness.

# POLLY AND Buster

## WHAT WILL HAPPEN NEXT?

Stay tuned for Polly and Buster's
next adventure!

Have you read
*The Wayward Witch
and the Feelings
Monster*, Book One
of the POLLY AND
BUSTER series?